His Orders

J. Raven Wilde

Copyright © 2019 J. Raven Wilde

Editing services provided by Kelly Hartigan at XterraWeb (editing.xterraweb.com).

Published by Twisted Crow Press, LLC

www.twistedcrowpress.com

ISBN: 979-8-9906871-0-3

Other Books by J. Raven Wilde

Standalone Novels

His Orders

Hot and Steamy Series

In Hot Pursuit

Hot Rod

One Hot Weekend

Falling For Series

Falling for the Rancher

Falling for the Cowboy

The Mummy's Curse Mini-Series

The Mummy's Curse Vol 1

The Sorcerer's Curse Vol 2

The Curse of Anubis Vol 3

The Mummy's Curse Mini-Series Box Set

Sanctuary Series

Claimed by the Alpha

The Omega and the Witch

The Rogue and the Rebel

Deerskin Peaks Series

Claimed by the Bear

Taming the Wildcat

For my friend Kay from *The Leaky Faucet*.

1

Sergeant Massey

I sat down the last of the boxes and let out a long sigh, wiping the sweat from my brow with the back of my hand. I took a moment to thank the movers before pausing in the entryway to assess my workload. The piles seemed nearly endless, but it was more bearable knowing I was only unpacking the necessities this trip. My enlistment was almost up, and I decided this would be my last assignment. I didn't feel the need to reenlist again. I had served my country long enough and felt it was time to become a civilian again. My time in the army had been somewhat enjoyable, but I wouldn't miss the abundance of male authority figures drunk on their own power. They had been a thorn in my side since my first day at boot camp.

After an hour of shuffling boxes around and sorting through most of my clothes and uniforms, I opted for a break. I took a quick shower, washing away the long day's work and letting the hot water give me a moment of relaxation, and slipped into a pair of jean shorts, a nice polo, and some strappy sandals I found in one of the boxes. This wasn't my first time being stationed here, but it had been a few years. I set out to see if my favorite hangout spot was still up and running. It was a bar and grill situated not too far from the base, yet just far enough away that not a lot of military personnel came here. They preferred the bars just outside the base's gates, and I preferred enjoying a quiet meal without a bunch of a rowdy meatheads egging each other on.

I smiled when I saw the familiar neon glow, and a warm nostalgia settled in my stomach when I walked through the doors to find not a thing had changed over the years. It was still a quieter place for anyone to walk in, enjoy a pay-per-view sporting event, and play pool or darts while enjoying a decent meal and a few cold drinks.

It was eight in the evening, and there were already a couple men lounging around the bar with glasses in their hands, a few younger guys playing a game of pool in the back room, and a couple of men and women sitting at tables and eating over to the far side away from the bar. It was a Monday night, and I hoped this was as big as the crowd would get. If history was any indicator, it would be a larger crowd come Friday night. It was typical for this place to be busy around pay-per-view nights, but the most I had ever seen was around fifteen people on a Friday night.

I'd brought a newspaper with me to read while eating my dinner, but I found my eyes darting between the paper and the baseball game on the big screen. I was about halfway through my burger and fries and on my second beer when I heard a man's voice talking close by me. It took me a few seconds to realize he was talking to me.

"I said can I buy you a drink?" said the voice with a little more force, and I zoned back into the bar. I turned towards the man, my eyes assessing him critically as I pursed my lips.

He wore a blue, faded Hawaiian print shirt half-tucked into his brown jogging pants and worn-out sneakers. He appeared to be in his late forties with dark eyes and even darker, unkempt hair. His patchy facial hair looked like he hadn't shaved in almost a week. His face was beaded with sweat, as if he'd run around the bar a few times before sitting down next to me. He was one of the two men sitting at the bar when I arrived. He had been hunched over a shot glass while the other man, still sitting over to the far right and nursing half a glass of something dark, had been watching the game on the TV.

"No, thank you," I said, shaking my head and turning back towards the TV. I was tired from moving and honestly just wasn't interested in having a conversation. The dinner was a nice break from unpacking, but it was only a short break, and I'd have to return to the mess of boxes soon.

"Come on," he slurred, his eyes half-lidded as he leaned towards me, giving me a hefty whiff of body odor and breath so saturated with alcohol it made my sinuses burn. "Just one drink, sweetheart… Maybe a walk outside."

My hands clenched into fists, and I gritted my teeth as anger flared in me. I *hated* that name. *Sweetheart, darling, sweetie, honey…* the pet names they called me when they gave me some demeaning task because of my gender or danced along the edges of a sexual harassment suit.

"I said no, I'm not interested." I shut him down curtly and jerked the newspaper back up to my face, hoping he would get the message.

He stood up unsteadily and leaned in again, jabbing his finger into my arm. "I think you're being pretty fucking rude." He paused before adding, "Bitch."

His foul odor swirled around my face again, and I winced and swallowed the urge to gag. Well, my dinner was ruined. The newspaper crumpled in my hands as I tensed, preparing to push the guy back and wind my arm up for a right hook, but before I could make the first move, someone chimed in from behind me.

"I think it's best if you left right now." The voice was gruff and commanding but held a deep warmth that sent a tingle up my spine. I watched the drunk stumble back a few paces as the man spoke again. "I said to leave."

Even I flinched at the loud command, fighting the instinct to leave myself. Four years in the army listening to barking orders and obeying them would do that to you. The drunk man hunkered down in the far corner of the bar, mumbling to himself. I let out a sigh of relief, the tension dissolving from my body, and turned to thank the good Samaritan, but he had already made his way back towards his spot at the bar. He swished the dark, amber liquid in his glass before taking a hearty sip. His gaze wandered back over to me and he gave me a nod. I raised my glass towards him, giving him an appreciative nod, before taking a drink.

"I could've handled that myself but thank you."

"I have no doubt you could've, but it's hard to enjoy the game while a woman is getting harassed a few feet away." He went back to watching the game, and I let the conversation die off.

I turned back to towards my food, but my eyes kept wandering back over to him, studying him. Generally, at five foot seven with a toned, athletic build, I was left to my own devices and didn't mind handling situations myself, but I appreciated his help. He diffused the situation well and kept me from disrupting the peaceful atmosphere. I liked coming here and preferred a low profile. The army didn't take kindly to soldiers beating up civilians — even if they were assholes.

The more I studied him, though, the more I began to appreciate the view. His hair was silver speckled with black and trimmed high and tight, which told me he was at least in his mid-to late forties. His well-defined, square jaw was clean shaven, and he had a slight tan which told me he spent time outdoors. He had large biceps, and his T-shirt pulled tight against his bulging chest. I couldn't help the slight arousal that jolted through me as my eyes traced the lines of his body. He was a fine specimen, for sure.

His eyes, now locked on me, were a piercing crystal blue. He was studying me just as I was him, and I felt my cheeks warm as a blush bloomed in them. I had been caught.

"I apologize for staring," I muttered before clearing my throat as I struggled to recover. "I was wondering if you were military?"

"Actually, yes, I am." His gaze leveled at me for a long moment before he spoke. "Are you as well?"

"Yes, sir. I just transferred back here. Got in a few hours ago and have a house full of moving boxes still waiting for me. I'm not supposed to report for duty until Thursday, but I was debating reporting in a little earlier. I don't do well with idle time."

He smiled, and I drew in a sharp breath. The lines of his face only made him more attractive, and I gave a shy smile in return.

"Dedicated, I like that. Never hurts to report in early. Where are you going?"

"Infantry." I shrugged. Since he was military, it was quite possible he was stationed at the same base as me. Or he could just be passing through, but I *really* hoped he was stationed here.

He raised his eyebrows in surprise. "Infantry? Really? Do you like what you do?"

His tone seemed genuinely curious, but I tensed up at the question. I didn't really like what I did in the army and wanted to do something else, but that wasn't really the kind of thing you told other people, especially those you don't know. In the army, it was all about the bureaucracy, titles, and ambition, and expressing dissatisfaction in your position without kissing your superiors' asses enough to earn yourself a promotion was looked down upon.

"No, I don't mind it," I lied, taking another drink of my beer. I spent four years in the infantry, doing three tours in the Middle East, and I was ready for a change of scenery. Most of those I knew had completed more tours than myself, and I felt like I was being selfish in saying that I had enough of the hot desert air and scorching sand, but I was. It was much harder overseas being a woman; the stereotyping and disrespect women get, thinking that we couldn't keep up with the men had begun to wear on my nerves.

"Ah, I can tell that you don't." He smirked, and I frowned. Maybe, it was the minuscule moment of pause before answering or he was an expert at reading body language. "I can pull some strings for you. Are you okay with desk duty?"

I cocked my head to the right, studying him and thinking it over. His expression was unreadable, and I wished I could understand his intentions. Sure, people had offered me favors in the army before, but I soon learned that every kind deed came with a price, usually twice the cost of the favor. People just didn't help others out of the kindness of their heart—unless they wanted a medal or something else entirely—and even then… But, I was only going to be in for another year, anyways. Desk duty wouldn't be that bad, and it would be nice for the change in pace. I shrugged my shoulders, keeping my tone nonchalant. "Sure, why not?"

Whatever he was planning—if he was planning something— would come out soon enough, and then, I'd pay the piper and go back to enjoying the civilian life.

He got off his stool and dropped a couple of bills on the bar. "Then report to Colonel Lang at 0800 hours tomorrow morning."

Without extending me another glance, he walked out of the bar, leaving me with more questions than answers.

Well, okay then. I huffed as my eyes lingered a little too long watching him leave, and I wondered if I made the right call. I took two more bites of my lukewarm burger and finished my beer before grabbing my newspaper, dropping a couple of bills for the tab, and then heading back towards my apartment to face the chaos.

Tomorrow would be an interesting day, for sure.

2

Sergeant Massey

By the time I had gotten checked in the following morning and found my way to Colonel Lang's office, it was precisely eight in the morning. I stepped inside a small office with an empty desk piled high with papers. I had expected a secretary to greet me, but I was met with silence. I wondered if I was meant to be the replacement, since the man at the bar, whose name I'd forgotten to grab, hadn't specified what kind of desk job.

I studied the room and ran my fingers over the files, glancing through the labels on the tabs, on the desk. It wasn't more than a few seconds later that the door to the right of the desk opened and startled me. Out stepped the man from the bar, and my stomach did a flip as a strangled cry escaped my lips. I never really paid much attention to my superiors in their uniforms, but I was at a loss of words as I drank him in. He filled out his camo fatigues perfectly, and my heart pounded in my ears.

"Did I scare you?" he asked, his eyes amused and a half-smile on his face. My gaze ran over the name tag stitched above his left pocket, and my eyes widened in realization. I quickly recovered and stood at attention.

"Colonel Lang, sir, Sergeant Massey reporting for duty." Immediately, I frowned as I realized I had forgotten to salute. Had he told me his name at the bar, maybe, I would have been more prepared. But it was hard for me to keep my thoughts in order with the way his uniform molded to his well-built form. As my thoughts and eyes wandered, I jerked back into my stiff pose, chastising myself for ogling my soon-to-be boss. If I kept this up, this would be my most difficult assignment yet.

"Sergeant Massey, you look surprised," he noted, his smile twisting into a boyish smirk that made my knees weak.

"Yes, sir, I didn't realize you were *the* Colonel Lang you were referring to at the bar…" I trailed off as his unnerving gaze rattled me.

"Well, you didn't ask." Humor sparkled in his eyes, and I realized he was enjoying playing with me. "But now, you know. My secretary transferred a week ago, and I've been having trouble finding a replacement. Being the CO, I figured I might as well snag someone transferring in."

His smile grew more devilish, and both arousal and fear rose within me, leaving me to question if I had made the right choice by saying yes to this position.

"Now," he continued, smacking his hand on the pile of papers. He was standing only a foot away from me, and I let out a shaky breath as I held his intense gaze. "As you can see, things are piling up — reports, letters, filing, you understand. I'll need you to organize these for me. I'll also need you to get coffee for my guests when they arrive for meetings, as well as have coffee made for me. You'll also need to remember a few addresses as you'll be picking up my dry cleaning and dropping them off at my house, as well as running other errands."

He handed me a pad of paper and a pen before abruptly breaking the stare and stalking back into his office. I didn't realize I was holding my breath until it wheezed out of me. It took me a moment to realize I was meant to follow him, and I stumbled after him. He picked up a piece of paper on his desk and handed it to me.

"The first address is my house, and the second address is the dry cleaners. You'll get my uniforms from my house on Monday mornings and take them to the cleaners. On Wednesday mornings, you'll pick them up and hang them in my closet. My bedroom is at the top of the stairs and to the left. There's only one closet, so it shouldn't be hard to figure out. Hang them on the far left."

I studied the paper, making mental notes and scribbling a few things onto my notepad. Didn't seem too hard. When I looked back up at him, my mind went blank. While I was writing everything down, he'd walked around his desk, placing his hands on the surface and leaning over to watch me. This posture did well to show off his muscular arms and broad shoulders. I gingerly bit my lip as I wondered what it would feel like to have those large hands all over my body and those strong arms pinning me against the wall, holding me up as he took me roughly. My gaze wandered up to his broad chest, and I almost sighed, wishing I could have just a tiny peek under those uniformed layers. After undressing him with my eyes, I made my way back up to his face and his bemused smile. I froze as I met his eyes, playful yet depthless.

"Any questions?" he asked, a slight bit of humor in his tone.

I cleared my throat as I glanced back towards my notes, jotting down some gibberish, and then clicked my pen. The embarrassment jumbled my thoughts, and it took me another moment to compose myself. "Uh, well, anything on the list that I need to do today, sir?" I avoided eye contact as I pretended to shuffle the papers in my hands. I could feel his gaze heavy on me still.

"Spend a few hours trying to learn the filing system and making your way through the stack of papers on the desk. Then, take the rest of the day off and learn where those addresses are as you'll need to know them. Wednesday, you'll need to pick up my dry cleaning. They open at 0830." He paused.

I glanced back up at him, meeting his eyes as he studied me more.

"Any *other* questions?" His crystal-blue eyes pierced into me and my heart skipped a beat.

"N-no, sir," I stammered before clearing my throat again. Why was I so unnerved? I'd dealt with plenty of men like him before, but none had so efficiently derailed me. He sat down in his chair and leaned back. Something about his expression flustered me, like he knew something I didn't and was more than willing to use that against me. This all seemed like a game to him. The way he moved and stared at me was meant to leave me squirming one way or another. Not telling me who he was at the bar just to see my reaction this morning? He was playing with me, plain and simple. I'd often been exposed to the games of military politics by which the higher-ups challenged each other, but I usually navigated the shark-filled waters carefully, trying not to venture too far from land. The way he was playing was dirty. Like a siren, he lured me away from the shore and towards the rocks far out to sea upon which I would sink myself into…and drown.

"Don't screw up, Sergeant I know it may be a bit more tasking than what you're used to, but it isn't a hard job."

I deadpanned and resisted the urge to roll my eyes. The condescension dripping from his voice could have drowned me, and a smart-ass comment made its way to the tip of my tongue. "No, sir. I won't screw it up, sir," I said instead, biting back the sassy response. The corner of his lips twitched as he contained a smirk, as if he sensed my thoughts, and he waved his hand to dismiss me.

I stormed back to my desk, abandoning the façade of professionalism for a moment as I huffed into my seat. I wasn't going to let him rile me up on the first day. I had never met a man who could so easily get under my skin who I still desired to get under my clothes.

It only took a moment to calm my nerves before I assessed the large stack of papers on my desk. I sensed something between us, a buzzing of tension that both enticed and alarmed me. I bet Mr. Salt-and-pepper, *sir*, felt it, too, but if he thought I was going to jeopardize the last year of my military career just to be another notch in his bedpost, then he had another thing coming.

I took a deep breath, trying to cool my hormones, and started sorting through the stack. It would help if he wasn't so damn hot. It would also help if I could scrounge up an ounce of control. This was going to be a long assignment if I had to tiptoe around every conversation with him in order to avoid mouthing off to my superior. My lack of self-restraint in that regard had gotten me into significant trouble in the past until I learned to keep my mouth shut. That's what I would do. I would keep the relationship strictly professional. I'd only speak to the colonel when absolutely necessary and keep myself busy in the meantime. Head low, spirits high, and I would survive the next three hundred sixty-five days without incident.

As I learned the previous secretary's filing system, I made a few adjustments before I had everything condensed into two piles which I labeled "to file" and "to type." Once I had made a good progress on the piles, it was about lunchtime and I stretched before hopping to my feet.

I met eyes with Colonel Lang, who had stood up at the same moment, and cursed internally. So much for avoidance. I knew it was immature of me in wanting to avoid my boss rather than face the problem head-on, but I hoped it was more mature than letting some comment slip and starting a whole other mess of problems for myself.

I waited for him to come out of the office in case he needed anything and gave a curt but polite nod as he held the door open for me. As we ruefully continued in the same direction, he tried to initiate small talk, but I kept my answers concise and respectful. When he realized I wasn't going to be much of a conversationalist, he changed his tactics.

"So, tell me, what made a woman like you interested in joining the army?" The way he emphasized "woman *like you*" made me tense up. I met his eyes and could see the amusement bubbling underneath the surface.

He was goading me, I knew that. He wanted a reaction out of me, but I couldn't put my finger on why. Though the base wasn't too bad when I had been stationed here years ago, I'd heard rumors that it had taken a turn for the worst when an influx of the dying regime of traditionalists moved in. Perhaps, he wanted to bait me into insubordination and then try to get me a one-way ticket out of the base. Perhaps, he wanted to trick me into sleeping with him and then ship me back off to infantry when he was done with me.

"It's the family business. I'm a legacy recruit.," I didn't bother to elaborate and kept my eyes pointed forward. The exit was within my sights, but it was still about fifty yards away.

He tried to bait me into playing with him again, but I skirted around the questions and deflected them despite the turmoil brewing in my mind. The way he looked at me as we continued walking in the same direction unnerved me. He had a smirk playing at his lips and an eyebrow raised as if asking. *So, this is how we're gonna play it?* I responded with a shamelessly blunt expression as if to answer: *Yes, sir, I don't have time for games, and if I can't control my tongue, I'm going to hold it.*

He walked me out of the building, and I could still feel his eyes on me as I stomped toward my car. I gritted my teeth as I slammed the door once I got in the car, and I gripped the steering wheel tightly in my frustration. As I watched him disappear into another section of the parking lot, I finally felt as if I was able to relax, and I let out a long sigh.

See? Not too hard at all.

3

Colonel Lang

I knew I shouldn't have given in to the urge to play with her. I had never been one for games. Not with politics, not with women, and especially not with an inappropriately young woman whom I'd hired on as my subordinate. It was a nearly impulsive decision and one that came with some sacrifice on my part to negotiate the staffing change. I would tell myself and anyone else who asked that I needed a new secretary and her arrival had been too convenient to pass up. However, deep down, I knew from the way she tensed at the bar—her body shifting its energy as she geared up for a fight—that she would get herself into trouble.

Over the past couple of years, a shift in management to an older male crowd had brought back a lot of the traditional views on a woman's role in the military. As a result, the number of female staff at the base had been reduced to staggeringly low numbers and left most units at the base a merciless boys' clubs. Women were unwelcomed and ridiculed and often bullied out of their positions. In several cases, damage control had to be brought in to sweep scandals and crimes by officials under the rug. It was sleazy and detrimental to the already rocky reputation of the army as a whole.

So, when I heard she was coming to the base as infantry, I'd felt a tad bit protective of her, and even deeper down, I felt selfish because I wanted her all to myself. There was something about her that intrigued me—that lured me into wanting to be closer to her. So, I made her my secretary, but from the moment I walked out of my office and saw her standing there, her fatigues flattering her every curve and her lips parted in surprise as she let out a strangled yelp, I realized I'd probably made a mistake.

Never had I ever considered hooking up with a subordinate, nor had I ever been interested in a woman this young before. All my past relationships had been with women no more than a few years younger than me. At this point, I had been in the army for twenty-two years, and I was far from being a fresh chicken. Though the years of training and disciplined moderation had made time kind to me, I still couldn't let myself forget I was nearly twice her age.

That thought had been moved to the back of my mind, though, when I'd walked her through her assignment. Every time she called me sir, my cock twitched. Every time I caught a glimpse of defiance in her eyes, I had a nearly overwhelming desire to dominate her. She was challenging me, and it made me more aroused than anything else. I could tell by the way she looked at me, her eyes tracing over my body, that if I wanted to take her, she'd give in. Even if not immediately, her resistance would wane until I had her. It wouldn't take much. However, I wasn't the kind of man who would take advantage of a woman like that. I wanted her to come to me, to ask me, to beg me to take her. So, I vented my frustration at not being able to have her by toying with her.

Despite her best attempts, her emotions splayed so obviously across her face that it left little doubt that my attitude was having an effect. When she was angry, the skin between her eyebrows puckered the tiniest bit. When I caught her checking me out, a flush spread over her cheeks and down her neck, disappearing beneath the collar of her shirt. I wanted to see how far it reached. I could picture her panting, the flush reaching the apex of her breasts, as she spread herself open for me and begged me to ravage her. I shifted my stance to try to hide the growing erection tenting my fatigues. If this was going to be my body's reaction to every one of our interactions for the next year, this office would be unbearable.

I quickly dismissed her and sat at my desk, trying to focus my mind on something more productive—or literally anything other than her. A clatter distracted me almost immediately, though, as she dropped a stack of files to the ground. She apologized before bending down to pick them up, offering me a hearty view of her ass. Against my better judgment, I did not get up to close the door but instead stared at her for far more time than appropriate. I suppressed the urge to groan, as her clothing stretched against her body, before putting my head in my hands to get my thoughts under control.

I finally managed to get some work done, but lunch rolled in faster than I expected. I stood up to head out and met eyes with Sergeant Massey, who had gotten up at the exact same moment. She seemed annoyed at the coincidence, and I smirked. I was driving her wild, and that was far more satisfying than I would have imagined. She waited for me respectfully, and I held the door out of my office open for her. When she walked past me, I caught a whiff of her scent—vanilla with a hint of coconut—and it left me aching. In my head, I pinned her against the wall, kissing her roughly without giving her a chance to protest. When she melted against me, I dragged her back into the office and had my way with her on top of the newly cleared office desk.

In reality, I filled the silence by prying into details about her—where she was stationed before, what kind of work she did, and how she ended up here. Her answers were very succinct, lacking any sort of detail or insight into herself. I switched up my tactics and tried teasing her again, but she kept her face impassive and her answers respectfully bland. It annoyed me that she'd shut herself off. Had I gone too far with my banter and just pushed her away? Then, I really looked at her face and realized the truth. It was taking every ounce of her self-control to hold her tongue.

I frowned as I realized what I was missing. She knew I was playing a game, but she didn't know why. I was used to being in a superior position, and my status afforded me the ability to say what I liked with little worry of consequence. In her, I had seen a contender, and I was baiting her to step up to the challenge. However, I forgot in my haste that her position was on a completely different level than mine. For her, she probably had learned early on to kiss ass or keep her head low but, whatever you do, don't talk back. I realized my error too late, and she had begun to question my intentions with moving her into my office.

I offered her a reprieve in the form of silence until we were out of the building and she was making her way to her car. I watched her go, devising a strategy for righting the wrong, but it seemed like the best way was to give her time. It was bold of me to assume we could build something so quickly, so I would give her time to adjust to this place, adjust to working for me, and then, in a couple of months, I would attempt to pursue her again.

For all I knew, the tension between us was just a passing fad. It was only fair to both of us to see if it would persist or if it would fade.

4

Sergeant Massey

It didn't take me long to relearn my way around town. My memory served me well from my time being stationed here before, but since it had been four years and only for a short stay, I printed out a map just to be safe.

Driving around, I saw plenty of new mixed in with the old, but it still had a familiar feeling to it. I found the places on my map with relative ease—it was a pretty small town, after all—and all that was left was to go to the colonel's house. I debated stopping by, but I decided against it as it was a bit inappropriate without having a real reason.

On Wednesday, I went to his house to drop off his dry cleaning. I stood outside for a moment pensively. I believed I remembered the colonel mentioning he had been stationed here for the better part of his career. However, his house was a very simple two-story lot and not at all what I thought an officer would choose to live in.

I briefly wondered if he shared his home with anyone, but I quickly squashed the thought as I did most of his errands and my first experience with him was insufferable enough that it was hard to believe he could possibly have a woman in his life. Plus, the way he looked at me. My body immediately grew hot at the thoughts, and I scolded myself as I went inside.

There were no pictures of family anywhere nor really any indication that this was a home more than a house set up simply for a real estate viewing. Standard furniture, standard floors, and standard wall paint. Nothing that gave any insight into the kind of person who would live here. His bedroom wasn't much better. His house looked like something out of a black-and-white IKEA catalog. It was simple and practical and completely lacking in personality. It was as pragmatic as I expected of a stereotypical, starched army man, but it left little to be picked up by my amateur detective skills.

What a lonely life, I thought, but I was hardly one to talk. Friends were hard to keep when you were constantly moving from assignment to assignment and forwarding addresses got lost in the mess of paperwork.

The longer I was in the army, the harder I found it to relate to other women and empathize with their struggles. Though I could dress up and fix my makeup with the best of them, I could also roll in the mud while dragging a much larger man to safety.

It was also for this reason that I found the dating scene hard. Men outside the army were often intimidated by a woman in fatigues with a few patches on her uniform. And don't even get me started on the men *in* the army. I had been there, done that, and it had left me hurting the past couple of years. I didn't have to touch the stove again to remember it was hot. I had no interest in dating again anytime soon. Mr. Salt-and-pepper wasn't going to change my mind about that even if my body tried to betray me.

I sighed as the air grew suffocating as my thoughts overwhelmed me. I made my way downstairs to the kitchen and scanned the counters and fridge for a list and found my first evidence that Colonel Lang had a history.

Pinned to the fridge was a discolored photo of the colonel in his much younger days. He had certainly aged well. Next to him stood two others, all standing, smiling, in their fatigues. I studied the photo for a long while, my eyes mesmerized by the soft features of my superior. He was cute back then, but he had aged into something rugged and sexy, something fierce and arousing. He was definitely more like wine and cheese, and with age, he had hit his prime.

I realized I had probably overstayed my welcome for just dropping off his dry cleaning. If I lingered any longer, he would come home to my scent, and while the thought of it filled me with warmth, I didn't want to push my luck. Plus, it felt creepy, and I didn't consider myself that kind of person. Especially not with my boss and commanding officer.

I left his house and made a stop to get us a couple of coffees before heading to work.

*****

"Sergeant," the colonel called loudly through the phone speaker, startling me.

I had been typing up notes from one of his previous meetings as well as a couple of letters to be sent out by the end of the day, and I had been working diligently for the past forty-five minutes undisturbed in the quiet office.

"Yes, sir?" I answered quickly.

"Get in here," he commanded, and my heart jumped to my throat at his clipped tone.

I had been working for the colonel for just over two months now, and I had a pretty good idea from the tone of his voice what to expect from our interactions. I wish I could say that time had dulled my reaction to his commanding voice and stature, but he still rattled my nerves. I also wished I could say I still didn't have inappropriate thoughts about my superior, but truly, it had only grown more intense.

The days in the office had gotten much more bearable, but at the same time, the tension was growing almost unbearable. Every passing glance left me wanting him and every brush of our skin as I handed him a report or passed a little too closely when he was holding the door open threatened to overwhelm me.

I scrambled to my feet with a pen and paper, expecting to jot down notes for a meeting I wasn't aware of or get scolded for mistyping something, and stepped into his office.

"I need you to pick up a few items for me: my shoes from Cobble Shoe Repair and my dry cleaning from the shop. Make sure they were able to get the stain out of the right cuff."

"Yes, sir," I replied, relieved he just seemed to be in a bad mood.

"Oh, and Sergeant"

I tensed and turned back—*here we go*—and found him staring at me with an unreadable expression.

"I need you to pick out a dress and some comfortable shoes for dancing."

I stared at him blankly as I processed what he said. After I replayed it a few times and he didn't give any indication of it being a joke, I furrowed my brows in confusion. "Excuse me…sir?"

"You're to attend the army ball this Saturday."

"Oh. No thank you, sir. I don't do balls and dresses and dancing." I declined, but his expression didn't change.

"I don't remember making this a request." His gaze was unwavering, and I tried to bite back the protest.

"Sir, please, I—" I squeaked, fumbling for an excuse and coming up empty.

I hadn't been to a dance since my senior prom in high school, and I had tripped over my own feet, ripping my dress and embarrassing myself in front of my whole class and their dates. Even worse was that my date joined in on the mocking and laughter rather than helping me up and offering me his jacket to cover myself up with. Since then, I've never bothered with any clubs or functions that had dancing on the list of activities.

"Sergeant, you're going to attend this ball, you're going to dance, and you're going to enjoy yourself. That's an order." His voice was sharp and demanding. He turned back to his work, signifying the end of the discussion.

I swallowed and cleared my throat, having felt it go dry. "Yes, sir," I whispered, backing out of the room and stepping around the corner as I took a moment to breathe.

My stomach churned at the thought of tripping over my feet in front of the colonel, in front of everyone. Anxiety quickened my heartbeat, as well as my breath for a moment, as I imagined a repeat of my complete embarrassment. I couldn't do that to myself. I couldn't make a fool of myself in front of the man I so desired. The oncoming panic attack continued brewing as I glanced into his office. He picked up the phone, and I took his distraction as an opportunity to escape to the bathroom.

5

Sergeant Massey

Lang gave me Thursday and Friday off to find myself a dress for the ball. It was originally only going to be Thursday, but after a lack of luck, he gave me Friday off, too. He suggested I drive to the next town and try there. I wondered if he could sense my reluctance and saw through my excuses not to go. I half-hoped I wouldn't find a dress that fit my standards, but at the second store I visited, I found a strapless black sheath dress that tapered to just below my knees. A slit exposed my right leg and left the fabric loose enough at the hem that it wasn't too difficult to walk in. I hated to admit it, but it fit all my criteria and I looked hot in it. So hot that I imagined the look Colonel Lang would have seeing me in it and was walking out of the door with it in a matter of minutes.

Next, I found a pair of flats to go with the dress that was the perfect combination of cute and practical. I considered myself too tall for heels and had no interested in pushing my luck with them.

Though I would never admit it out loud, excitement gripped me tightly with anxiety at the thought of the ball tomorrow.

Feeling luxurious, I scheduled a hair and nail appointment for Saturday morning. They helped ease my nerves a little, but by early afternoon, I was all ready to go and had hours of idle time before it was time to head to the ball. If I wasn't already looking my best, with my hair curled delicately around my face and my makeup highlighting my features, I would have gone for a run to burn off some steam. However, the empty space in my schedule left room for anxiety to creep in at full force, and I decided to have a drink to dull my thoughts.

One drink turned into two and then three, and by the time I had to leave, I had to get a taxi to drive me to the ball. Nausea still plagued me, and I felt out of place in my dress and makeup. I didn't see the colonel when I arrived, which left me circling the room, sticking close to the outer edges of the crowd, trying to keep out of sight and mind of the others.

Finally, I situated myself in a corner near the exit and passed the time smoothing out wrinkles in my dress that didn't exist. I knew it was an anxious maneuver, but as the night grew older, it was doing little to calm my racing mind and the lights had become a tad bit blurry.

I had debated passing the bar for another drink, but I already had doubts at my ability to speak clearly and I knew I was only one drink away from making a drunk mess of myself. The best plan was to continue scanning the crowd to report what I saw come Monday and wait for the appropriate time to make my exit.

When most of the venue had filled with people and their dates, I desperately looked for the colonel, but my combing of the dance floor, the bar, and all the faces sitting at the tables yielded no results.

The tension in my shoulders began to relax, and I released a long breath. Relief crept in shadowed by disappointment. I wouldn't have to see him and risk embarrassing myself, but also, I was really hoping he would get to see me in this dress.

Thinking that I had been there long enough, I turned the corner towards the exit and ran right into someone. I opened my mouth to apologize as I stepped back to let them through when his face came into focus, and my heart and stomach simultaneously ached. I had run right into the colonel.

"You made it," he said, a soft smile on his lips as his eyes met mine. He must have noticed the surprise and alarm. "Ah, were you trying to run away?"

"N-no, no, sir. I was only headed to the ladies room to freshen up." I shook my head, smiling, and my eyes wandered lower, taking him in. *Oh, damn, he looks finer in his dress uniform,* I thought.

He smirked as if he could read my thoughts and I barely held myself steady as I swooned. I noticed the way his eyes undressed me, and my smile faltered as my body temperature rose a few degrees. Nervousness caused me to fidget, and I began to fan myself. The alcohol was heavy on my mind, and I knew control wasn't my strong suit right now.

"Here, have a drink; it'll calm your nerves." He handed me a glass, and I took it without thought. A dark amber liquid mingled with the ice, and I figured a sip wouldn't hurt.

"Come dance with me," he asked.

I took a test sip, and I choked. A bitter liquid ran over my tongue as I quickly swallowed. Feeling brave, I took a larger sip. Fortunately, it soothed the need to cough, and I set the glass on the table.

"Excuse me, sir?"

His dark eyes locked on me as he raised an eyebrow at the glass, now over half empty. Whatever it was, it was strong. I could still feel the burn of the alcohol on my tongue and throat. Warmth spread throughout my stomach, and it stopped flipping for a moment.

"I said dance with me," he breathed, grabbing my hand and leading me towards the dance floor. A voice in the back of my mind screamed in protest, and I started to form an excuse, but he was already prepared. "No need to powder your nose. You look lovely."

His ability to predict what I was about to say was unnerving. He didn't wait for a response this time and simply grabbed my arm and gently pulled me out onto the dance floor.

He swung me around, casually pulling me into him, until I was pressed against him. He slid one hand to the small of my back, and with the other, he grabbed mine and began to sway us back and forth.

I placed my other hand on his shoulder and drew in a sharp breath at the firm, hard muscles under my grip. They tensed as my fingers brushed them, and I glanced up into his eyes. He was staring at me with an expression that I couldn't quite place, but it made me feel tingly between my legs. My heartbeat quickened its pace and with it came a hypersensitivity.

He smelled wonderful, a mixture of expensive cologne and musk. I took in a deep breath, enjoying his scent, and let it clear my thoughts of running. My body temperature rose higher, and I began to feel slightly dizzy. He moved his hand lower, to the base of my spine, and I shuddered against him, my breaths shaky as I stared up at him with wanting eyes.

As we swayed with my chest pressed against him, the fabric brushed against my nipples, and I resisted the urge to moan. I had made the choice not to wear a bra, and now, I was paying for it.

His body was so warm, his hot breath tickling my cheek as he leaned in and brushed his lips against the top of my ear and whispered, "I'm so glad you made it tonight. For a moment, I didn't think you were going to show."

You ordered me to be here, I thought, but then, by the surprised look in his eyes as he pulled away, I realized I had said it out loud.

After a moment's recovery, he chuckled and pulled me back against him. My brain stopped working as his fingers stroked the base of my spine, and I wondered if it was me or the room that was roasting.

As his face rubbed against my hair, jolts of electricity shot through me from every point of contact, and I could feel myself growing wetter with every moment. I closed my eyes, enjoying the sensations he was sending through my body. I wanted him more than anything. I cared little for everyone who was watching. If he wanted to rip the cloth and decorations off a table and fuck me here, I would offer little resistance. The brush of his lips against my ear was so sensual that my grip tightened on him.

I resisted the urge to ask him to take me somewhere private. I wanted him to go further, to explore my body with those hands and that mouth of his. I wanted to see what hid beneath that uniform. I wanted to run my hands across the bulging muscles of his chest and down his abdomen until I reached my destination. I wanted my lips to follow in pursuit of my hands. I wanted to know what he tasted like.

I drew in a deep breath at the thought, the dizziness causing me to rock in his arms. I was shamelessly lusting over my boss at this moment. These past two months had been brutal every time I stepped into his office to see him. Since day one, I wanted to slam the door and spread myself on his desk as I begged him to take me.

A single thread of dignity held together my resistance, but every day was a fight.

Between our clothing, I felt his cock twitch, as if he heard every little thought in my mind and was thinking the same thing, and I let out a small whimper. His grip tightened on me, and I could have sworn I heard a groan in my ear as he pressed his cock into me.

In the back of my mind, I prayed to the universe that no one was paying attention to us. We had ventured far out of the realm of appropriate—the superior and his subordinate, the officer and his secretary. There was a whole section in the rule book forbidding this kind of fraternization.

The song finally came to an end, and he released me slowly. Like a breath of fresh air, my mind was clear for a moment, and a tremendous wave of thoughts barreled into me. I could feel his eyes on me, but I couldn't meet them as I turned quickly and dashed off to the restroom without another glance. A chill settled into me at being away from him, and I shuddered.

In a bit of a haze, I found my way down the hall and into the ladies room, locking myself in the last stall and collapsing against the cool wall and floor. I had to sit down, my head was spinning with the room, and I was thankful for the coolness of the wall pressing against my back, which helped soothe me.

I closed my eyes and lowered my head to rest on top of my knees. My legs were shaking, and my core was throbbing in need for release. I had a powerful urge to touch myself, but the sound of female voices chattering at the sinks reminded me it was a public restroom and it would have to wait until later.

How could one feel so turned on and nauseated at the same time?

Several minutes later, my breath evened out and my heartbeat calmed. A toilet flushed next to my stall and reminded me that the world around me was still in motion.

I was feeling slightly better with the cool tiles bringing my body temperature down to normal levels again. My legs stopped shaking, and the throbbing between them had nearly disappeared. I was exhausted and just wanted to go home.

I stood up slowly, steadying myself against the wall as my knees trembled. I needed to get home and away from Colonel Lang ASAP. How had I allowed myself to lose control like that?

I walked out of the stall to find the bathroom thankfully empty. I splashed cool water on my face, ignoring my makeup, and dried my face with a paper towel. When I left the bathroom, my stomach flipped as I looked up and saw Colonel Lang standing several feet away with alarm on his face. He stepped up to me and brushed a strand of hair behind my ear. "Oh, Massey, I'm so sorry. Let me get you home."

Without waiting for a response, he wrapped an arm around my back and ushered me out the door, shielding me from the crowd still dancing and mingling in the ballroom. He helped me into the passenger seat of his car and secured my seat belt before getting behind the wheel and taking off. I leaned my head back and closed my eyes. Exhaustion pulled me under as I gave in to the warm embrace of sleep, not realizing I never gave him my address.

6

Colonel Lang

She was simply stunning.

From across the ballroom, my eyes locked on her, and I stood frozen in awe. She wore a strapless black dress that accentuated her curves with a slit exposing the upper skin of her thigh. I needed to get a closer look.

She stood in the shadows, pressed tightly against the wall, tucked away from everyone else. Even from this far away, I could tell she was nervous and fidgeting. I started to make my way over to her. She looked about to dart out, and I quickly grabbed us each a bourbon from the bar as I made my way towards her. I didn't even know if she liked bourbon, but she looked like she could use a drink.

I tried to stick to the shadows as much as I could as I moved toward her. I had already been stopped and dragged into conversations nearly ten times just on my way into the ballroom. Now that I had my eyes on the prize, I didn't want any distractions.

Halfway to her, I heard someone call my name, but I quickly spun into the hallway to avoid them. It was rude, sure, but I had a destination and a one-track mind. I didn't want a conversation. I wanted her.

To put it frankly, these past few months had been torture. Once I backed off, our relationship became much less volatile, but it was boring. She performed her tasks dutifully and made pleasant small talk, but it felt like both of us were holding back.

When she thought I wasn't paying attention, I'd notice her watching me. When I glanced her way, she reddened and got back to her work. I felt hyperaware of her at every instance. I thought throwing myself into my work would help, but she was always waiting in the back of my mind for the moment my focus wavered.

I imagined us both in so many ways, so many positions. Sometimes, it was unbearable. Sometimes, I left work a little bit earlier just to take care of an erection that wouldn't go away. Sometimes, I swear she was doing things just to drive me crazy— bending over to pick up something from the floor, leaning over her desk to grab something at the far end, and working in a tight-fitting, translucent white shirt while waiting for her uniform to dry after she spilled coffee on it. I consider myself a strong man, but that last one almost broke me.

As I turned the corner to see her, I met bright eyes, wide with surprise as she had gotten caught trying to leave. I couldn't keep the smile off my lips— *Gotcha!* She stammered out an excuse, and her anxiety was so obvious it hurt. I handed her a drink in hopes it would calm her nerves. She seemed much more at ease with the glass, so I took a chance and asked her to dance. She was mid-sip when she choked and ended up swallowing most of it. It pained me to watch the one-hundred-fifty-dollar bourbon gulped like that, but I was much more concerned with Nicole who had put a hand on the table to steady herself. She stood straighter after a moment and met my eyes, her dark lashes framing hers in such a seductive fashion that I was ready to take her home right then. She was irresistible.

I needed her against me at that moment, so I took her arm and pulled her with me to the dance floor. I was going to keep us an appropriate distance apart, but the way her body melded against mine as she leaned into me made me hold her possessively. Reputation be damned, I wanted to touch her and feel her and get to know every inch of her.

My cock bulged as she rubbed against me, and she let out a soft gasp of pleasure as my hand slid farther down her back. I suppressed a groan as I pushed against the small of her back, letting her feel how hard she made me through our clothes. She met my eyes, and in them, I saw the same desire and want that was possessing me. Both of us ready to throw caution to the wind and lose ourselves right here. I was tempted to ask her if she wanted to go back to my place, or hell, I'd settle for an empty room somewhere.

The song ended, but before I could get a word out, she excused herself and dashed away. I went after her, ignoring a few of my colleagues who tried to stop me and make some sort of idle chatter. She disappeared into the bathroom, and I stood outside to wait and worry.

Several groups of women went in and out of the bathroom, delivering some passing—and some lingering—glances as they walked by. I retraced my steps, trying to figure out where I fucked up, and prepared an apology. Perhaps, I was too pushy. Perhaps, I had misread her signals. Perhaps, I was the last person she wanted to see right now, but I had to come clean to her.

When she finally walked out, I noticed the sheen of sweat on her hairline and the fuzzy look in her eyes. I realized my mistake. She had been drinking long before I handed her the bourbon.

Another group of women approached the bathroom and I quickly wrapped my arm around her, directing her toward the exit. She swayed in my arms, but I kept her steady until I had her safely buckled into my passenger seat. Inside, I was seething.

I was the one who had pressured her to come tonight. I thought she was being shy and antisocial, so I ordered her to. Whatever had happened in the past, it was enough to push her to drink like this. I'd seen her have a few beers before, but she was still right on her feet. She must have gone all out for this occasion.

My fingers gripped the steering wheel so tightly my knuckles turned white. I turned to ask her where she lived, but she was already asleep, her soft breathing fogging up the passenger window. I watched her for a moment as I calmed down. She was so serene it left my heart aching. I realized then that it wasn't just my body that wanted her.

I drove us to my house carefully, trying not to wake her. When I got home, I gently carried her into the house and laid her on the couch. I thought about bringing her upstairs, but it was a difficult journey, and I worried about knocking her head on something. Also, I thought a stranger's couch was a little bit less scary than waking up in a stranger's bed…especially after a night of blacking out.

I stripped off her shoes and covered her with a blanket. I left her a glass of water, an aspirin, and a carefully written note about where she was, and for good measure, I added a comment about the dangers of alcoholism and public intoxication.

I watched her for another moment as she slept. I wondered what could have possibly led her to endanger herself like this. What happened in her past that left her hurting so much? I was much farther from knowing and understanding Nicole than I thought. She let out a soft whimper in her sleep as she turned over and pulled the blanket up around her. I took this as my cue to leave but made a mental note to question her about it tomorrow.

It took me a while to get to sleep as I lay in bed, staring up at the ceiling. Mixed emotions swirled within me. One, I felt angry with myself for not reading more into her apprehension at going to the ball. Two, I was angry with whoever had wronged her in the past which contributed to her anxious reaction. Three, my mind kept steering towards entirely inappropriate thoughts about the woman passed out on my couch downstairs. Once I convinced my body we would *not* be jerking off to an unconscious person, I finally was able to give in to sleep.

7

Sergeant Massey

I woke up to the smell of bacon and eggs. It was an unusual scent, considering my breakfast usually consisted of coffee, hold the cream and sugar. I stretched out in bed, enjoying the scent, before realizing the texture beneath my body was all wrong.

My eyes snapped open to find myself in a completely unfamiliar place. Well, unfamiliar for the first couple of moments until I recognized the bland, catalog furniture. It was Colonel Lang's house. I jerked to my feet, bumping into the table and knocking something onto the floor. I let out a startled yelp as something cold and wet soaked my feet. I looked down and saw an empty glass over a dark spot on the rug. The thud caused Colonel Lang to rush into the room, and we both stared at each other in surprise.

He was dressed in a pair of jeans and a plain white T-shirt. The shirt molded tightly to his muscles, and I don't think jeans have ever looked so good. A dishtowel was thrown over his shoulder, and it added an erotically domestic twist on the handyman look. I noticed his eyes were not on my face, and I looked down to see my dress had ridden up quite a bit and the slit on my thigh was now above my hip, revealing the stringy black lace panties I wore underneath.

I blushed darkly as I pushed the fabric of the dress back down. The colonel seemed to recover as he cleared his throat, pulled the towel off his shoulder to dry his hands, and glanced back towards the kitchen to give me a moment of privacy.

"Oh, uh, sorry, I spilled some water on your floor," I apologized, crossing my arms uncomfortably over my chest. I was wearing the dress from last night but was a lot less comfortable standing here in his living room.

"It's all right. A little water never hurt anything. Here." He tossed me the towel. "Breakfast is almost ready; I'll go grab you a shirt. You look cold."

As he disappeared, I felt a warm, appreciative feeling in the pit of my stomach. He seemed to have a knack for that—for knowing when I needed something. It was unnerving sometimes, how he seemed to read my thoughts, but in moments like this, it just made me feel all tingly.

I got down onto my hands and knees on the floor and began pressing the towel into the wet spot. I heard a noise behind me and turned to see the colonel standing at the bottom of the stairs. He held a T-shirt in his hand and a wildly hungry look in his eyes. I bit my lip as I followed his eyes to my ass. I noticed the bulge against the front of his jeans and a hot feeling rose within me.

I sat up on my knees to hide my smile. I caught him checking me out. I knew it wasn't the first time as I had teased him enough, feigning clumsiness in order to give him a sneak peek, but I had never so blatantly seen him shamelessly enjoying the view. My thoughts came to an abrupt halt when he tossed the T-shirt over my head. I chuckled as he called out, "Breakfast's ready."

I stood up and pulled the shirt over my head. It was a far stretch from a comfortable pair of jeans and tennis shoes, but I felt kind of hot in his T-shirt, though I knew he was just being a gentleman.

I walked into the kitchen, and he gave me an appraising look. I could tell he appreciated my outfit as his gaze ran up and down me. I took a seat at the table as he handed me a plate of scrambled eggs and bacon. I took a whiff and sighed. It smelled delicious, and my stomach rumbled.

He studied me from the other side of the table with a plate of his own. "So, was it me that led you to drinking?" I paused, about to shovel the eggs into my mouth and frowned.

"Excuse me, sir?"

"Do I make you nervous? You ended up getting pretty drunk last night. I wondered if it had anything to do with me."

The intensity of his eyes prompted me to set down my fork. "It wasn't so much you as it was the atmosphere. I don't do dances or balls or any of that. I haven't been to anything like that since senior prom, and that was enough for me."

He raised an eyebrow in surprise. "Care to elaborate?"

"No, thank you."

He seemed to be debating with himself whether or not to push the issue. I couldn't resist the urge to eat anymore, so I took a bite of the eggs.

A surprisingly good cook, I noted as I began shoveling food into my mouth. It was actually delicious—I took another bite—*really* delicious. Who knew scrambled eggs could taste like this?

I suppressed the urge to moan until I took a bite of the bacon. It was the perfect amount of crispy without being blackened. It melted in my mouth, and I couldn't resist myself. I moaned. I froze after I made the noise and glanced up at him. He was watching me with dark, erotic eyes that made my body temperature rise.

"So, do you have a man in your life?"

His question was so direct that I swallowed the partially chewed bacon and ended up in a coughing fit as I tried to dislodge it from my throat. He handed me a cup of coffee, and I downed a sip too quickly, wincing as it scorched my mouth. I took a deep breath and another sip of coffee only to want to spit it back out. I looked down at the murky, creamy liquid in horror.

"What is in this coffee? Can this even be called coffee?" My nose wrinkled up in disgust.

The Colonel chuckled. "Sorry, I thought most women your age preferred sweeter things. I wasn't actually sure how you took your coffee."

"Black as can be, thank you very much. I need a wake-up, not a dessert," I scoffed, and he smirked.

"Noted." He took the glass and dumped it down the sink, before pouring me a new one.

"You didn't answer my question," he said as he handed me the new glass.

I hesitated, biting my lip. "Er…no, there's no man in my life." His eyes were so focused on me it left me frazzled, and I looked down at my hands tightly wrapped around the coffee mug.

"Is this intentional or…" I shrugged, sipping on the coffee.

He leaned towards me. "Or is it your problem with authority?"

My eyebrows rose at his question as I met his eyes. "Why would you say that?"

"Just the way you hold yourself." He reached his hand out, lifting my chin so I was forced to keep looking at him. "The defiant look in your eyes whenever I give you an order. The challenging way you set your jaw, like you're always holding back some comment. I always want to know what's going on inside that head of yours."

I parted my lips in surprise. Was I really that obvious? His eyes locked on my mouth, and he brushed his thumb across my bottom lip, and I trembled. My bottom lip tingled, and I became aware of the growing arousal between my legs.

"Well, I wouldn't say I had a problem with authority…" I trailed off when he pulled his hand away, narrowing his eyes.

"Don't lie to me," he demanded roughly.

I glared at him, gritting my teeth. "Okay. Fine, you're right. I have a problem with men thinking that women are just servants to be ordered around and objects to be used. I have no problem obeying the orders of my superiors, but every man in the army, regardless of rank, seems to think themselves entitled to be my superiors. Privates trying to hand off their cleaning duties to me because 'I'm a woman and that's what we're there for.' Superiors making inappropriate comments and trying to wheedle me into impossible situations. I'm tired of being treated differently than my male counterparts when we're both capable of the same work."

"What made you want to join the army then?" he asked. I narrowed my eyes, and he put up his hand defensively. "I don't mean that to offend. I'm genuinely curious. It's no secret that sexism runs rampart."

I cooled down a little and shrugged. "My dad was in the army. He met my mom while he was enlisted, and they had me. I was an only child, so I was treated as both the son and daughter. We moved a lot growing up when he was assigned at different bases, but then, he got stationed in the Middle East during the Iraqi War and… Well, he came home with a flag draped over him."

"I'm sorry for your loss." His voice was soft and soothing. He reached out a hand as if to place over mine before having second thoughts and pulling it back.

"He died a hero. My father believed in this country. He believed in the military, and he believed serving was the greatest honor. My fondest memories were when my mom and I were invited onto the base with him. He was always so proud of his job and what the country was doing. My favorite picture of him growing up was him in his officer's uniform with all his stripes and medals in front of the flag. He has this expression that just takes your breath away."

"So, is this what you meant by the family business?"

"Sort of. I wanted to follow in his footsteps, but he never wanted me to. He wanted me to go to college and get a good job. He wanted me to experience the benefits of the life that he fought to protect. Perhaps, he knew something that I didn't know.

"I tried living his dream, and I applied for a bunch of colleges, but my grades and our finances didn't really make it feasible, so instead, I followed what I thought was my dream, which was being just like my dad. I worked hard through boot camp to be near the top of my class, but while the men around me were shooting through the ranks, I stagnated at sergeant

"When I tried pushing to know why, they started moving me around before finally just shipping me overseas. A couple years of being led in circles, and now, I'm just trying to keep a low profile until my enlistment ends."

I stopped, surprised by how open I became with him. I hadn't told anyone this much about me in a long time, and the last person I had gotten this intimate with betrayed the trust I had given him. Panic rose within me at the thought of going through that again, and just as quickly as the walls had come down, I built them back up. Colonel Lang's gaze never left me, but he looked thoughtful now, somber.

"Finish up your breakfast, and I'll take you back home." He stood up and left me alone. I ate in silence. The food was still good but had cooled significantly in the time we spent talking. So had the coffee.

He returned in running clothes as I was finishing the last bite in running clothes. I raised my eyebrows in surprise at the change—and at how incredibly sexy he looked in them—and he told me he felt the need to go for a run and there was a trail not too far from the base. If I wasn't so hungover, I would have asked to join him. My bed and a good book sounded much more enticing at the moment than exercise.

We were quiet most of the ride to my place. His expression gave nothing away, and it just left me more anxious. Was he plotting how to use my words against me or my story to manipulate me? Did he think I was pathetic for giving up on my dream? My mind was still racing as frantically as my heartbeat when he finally pulled up outside my building.

"Hey, Sergeant," the colonel called when I was halfway to the doorway, and I turned back towards him. "Please don't give up on men just yet."

8

Sergeant Massey

His words were still on my mind as I settled into bed, freshly showered and dressed in only pajama shorts and his T-shirt. I would have to wash it and give it back to him eventually, but it was comfortable and made me feel safe.

Our conversation replayed itself in my mind, and I started to dread the thought of going to work on Monday. He seemed to read me like a book, but I had absolutely no idea what was going on in his head. Sometimes I thought I had him figured out, but then, he'd do something that completely threw me off my game.

At the ball, he seemed so into me, but then I had laid out the better part of my life story for him, and it'd made him pensive and closed off. It made me feel vulnerable and confused.

"'Don't give up on men just yet.'" What did that mean? Was he interested in me? Did he know someone interested in me? Was he just telling me platonically that I was too young to give up on relationships? I set down my book, and I covered my face with my pillow and groaned as I squirmed in the sheets.

Mr. Salt-and-pepper was an enigma that would single-handedly be my doom. Was this another one of his games, or was he actually interested?

I was driving myself crazy thinking about it. I needed to get laid, desperately. It had been a couple years, and while I could take care of myself, there were aspects of human intimacy that could not be replicated using a piece of silicone.

I wondered if he would be willing to help me relieve some of the built-up sexual frustration that had been compounding in me for a while.

I hummed pleasantly as I imagined the colonel having his way with me. I could come clean to him about my feelings, but they were jumbled up incoherently enough in my thoughts I doubted I'd be able to form them into words. There was no question that I was attracted to him, but it was so inappropriate I didn't know where to start.

I huffed and stuffed my face into my pillow again. I was playing a dangerous game. If I told him how I felt and he didn't return my feelings, I could way overstep and shatter the already fragile working relationship we had going. Also, it was highly frowned upon for superiors to have relations with their subordinates. They were pretty common, but if they went awry, the women usually got the short end of the stick.

Still, my mind was caught up on circling the idea that the risk could possibly be worth the reward. I was never usually one for just sex, but I had a feeling it was the safest option here. If I just held on to the physical attraction, then it wouldn't be nearly as intimidating if he turned me down. While, if he ended up wanting to have sex, we could start with a one-night stand and maybe transition into friends with benefits if it worked out well. Then it was just two consenting adults releasing their frustration. Low stress, low emotional attachment, and low risk if we decided to break things off.

I couldn't believe I was actually considering pursuing this. I made the conscious decision to be less subtle in my flirtations and more direct with my feelings. I was tired of playing games; I was ready for something real.

For some reason, the thought of pursuing a relationship with him made me even more anxious about seeing him. My nerves didn't give me a break until I pulled into his driveway the next morning to find his SUV already gone.

I let out a long sigh of relief. It was prolonging the inevitable, but it gave me a little longer to prepare myself. I picked up his dry cleaning and dropped it off before picking up coffee and muffins for the "office." I took my time pulling into the base until I couldn't put off the inevitable any longer.

When I got to the office, he was on the phone. I drew in a deep breath and walked in. I set his coffee on the desk, and he glanced up at me. He pointed to a stack of papers on the desk, which I noted were a stack of notes for me to type as I swept them up. My heart didn't stop racing until I was seated at my desk with the door to the colonel's office shut, muffling his voice.

The rest of the week went by without incident. Mostly because he had meetings nonstop, so we saw very little of each other. Most of his meetings were too high clearance for me to attend and keep notes for him, so I ended up having a bit of free time during the days. He seemed in a sour mood overall, and I hoped he didn't notice my nervousness with the few interactions we had.

He was in and out all week until Friday when I found a note on my desk with a pile of papers asking me to clear my lunch plans because he was taking me out. The note was enough to disturb my whole morning, and the time I should have spent doing my job I instead spent hyper-analyzing the potential meanings of this lunch.

When lunch finally came around, I had circled enough scenarios that I considered myself prepared for everything—from getting fired to passionate office sex. Of course, my overactive imagination far exceeded reality, but I still found myself unprepared when he showed up just before noon to escort me to lunch.

9

Colonel Lang

I was relieved when Friday finally rolled around, and I had a moment to breathe. I still had a morning meeting, but it was the last in the marathon, and then, I had the afternoon to catch up on my work. It also gave me time so that I could finally have a chance to sit down with Nicole. I had ended our conversation rather abruptly on Sunday before driving her home because my thoughts had gone out of control. I knew I wanted her before, but the feeling got so much deeper when she told me about her past. I felt raw and angry after she told me about her father's pride in our organization and then how she'd been slighted. She deserved better, and it angered me that my colleagues and I were not able to give it to her.

I went for a run to blow off the steam that was building inside me, and then, I decided I was going to pursue her. After the dance on Saturday and listening to her open up Sunday, I needed closure.

I needed to figure out if she was interested in me, and if she was, I needed to get lost in her. I was tired of playing cat and mouse; I was ready for something real.

Unfortunately, my plans were brought to a screeching halt when I walked in Monday to a manufactured crisis that had been blown wildly out of proportion. After a series of nonstop meetings to douse the fires, damage control was finally complete, but only after four and a half days.

On Friday, I got in early, left the note on her desk before heading out to another meeting, and then returned to the office just before noon to pick Nicole up.

She looked nervous when I finally got in, but it was still such a relief to see her. I had been uptight most of the week, frustrated with my colleagues for a plethora of reasons, so I hadn't had much time to appreciate her.

Now that she was standing in front of me, I paused to drink her in. It felt like I had finally released the breath I had been holding. My entire body relaxed, and I barely resisted the urge to go and wrap my arms around her. I'd never been one to seek the comfort of a woman's arms to relieve a stressful day, but with her, it felt like I needed it.

"Are you ready to go, Sergeant? I need a burger and a beer," I told her, and she jumped up, grabbing her purse and jacket.

"Is that a half day for you then, sir?" she asked, a hint of humor in her voice, and I held back a smile.

"We'll see."

I held the door open for her, and she walked past, brushing by me closely. I got a whiff of her scent, and her shoulder brushed against my chest. She mumbled an apology, but in her eyes sparked a mischief that caused my cock to twitch. I suppressed a groan as I walked after her. It felt like she was playing with me, but I was willing to play back.

Once in the car, I turned the key in the ignition and glanced towards her. "Last time you were sitting in that seat, you were drunk and out cold."

"Yeah, well, I paid the price for that Sunday. Plus, it seems you'll never let me forget it."

I smirked at how red her face became and put the car in gear. "I'll certainly never forget that dress."

She gave me a hot, long stare, and I tightened my grip on the wheel. It was hard not to want to just drop the appearances and take her back to my place. It had been a long week and I could use a long night with a beautiful woman, but it would have to wait until I was completely certain about Nicole's feelings.

I pulled into a small burger joint, and when we walked inside, I paused to take a deep breath of the soothing scent. Grease and BBQ sauce. It smelled like home.

Once we were seated, I studied Nicole for a moment, before folding my hands in front of me and leaning towards her. "So, did you have a nice week, Sergeant?"

She raised an eyebrow. "It was a little boring, actually."

"Did you miss me?"

"Well, I wouldn't say that." She looked down, the corner of her lip twitching into a smile. Her eyes fluttered back up to me for only a moment before looking back toward the menu. "But it is fair to say that the office is a little better with you there."

I couldn't stop the smile from spreading across my lips, so I picked up the menu to hide it. I watched her over the top, admiring her for a moment, while she was occupied. She glanced up at me and saw me watching her. She was absolutely stunning. I don't know how she was able to be single for this long. Surely, men were pursuing her in droves. Was she simply bored?

"I want you to be honest with me, Nicole," I began, and her eyes widened in a fleeting moment of panic. I accidentally used her first name, but I continued. "Why are you single, really? Even having an issue with authority, it seems a bit farfetched to call off all men."

The humor in her face immediately disappeared, and she closed the menu and crossed her arms, closing herself off as well. She pursed her lips and studied me for a minute. I worried I had far overstepped the line, but after a moment, she spoke.

"Do you really want to know?" she asked, and I frowned at the intensity of her expression but nodded.

Before she could continue, the waitress brought our drinks and took our orders. Once we were alone, she took another long pause. I began to get worried and was about to assure her she was under no obligation to tell me, but then, she launched into her story.

"It wasn't men as a whole that put me off relationships, just one man did it.

"A little over two years ago, I was stationed in Afghanistan on my first tour. There was another sergeant from my class there, and we hit it off immediately. We both were driven soldiers and thrived off challenging each other. One of the ranking officers was looking for someone to fill a position that would be quite a promotion for anyone. We both ended up trying for it.

"I began to see his true colors as the competition grew tighter. He started manipulating me and the other officers, anything to put himself ahead. He ended up sabotaging my chances at the promotion and backed me into a corner, blackmailing me so I wouldn't break up with him when I realized the monster he was.

"He didn't end up getting the promotion either, and he took out his frustration on me. First, in words, but then, it started to get physical. I tried to leave him a few times, but there was nowhere to go. There's not a lot of support for women over there, as you'd probably expect for the Middle East. The army was no help in the matter either. Over there, soldiers can get away with a lot, men especially.

"I thought I could just bide my time until my assignment ended, and then, I'd be able to escape him. Finally, my tour was over, and I planned to go back to the US, but he sabotaged my reassignment so he could keep me with him.

"He only became more ruthless and manipulative as time went on, and I thought the abuse would never end, but he ended up getting a promotion and a ticket back to the states, and he took it, leaving me behind. It got a lot more bearable after he was gone. I did a third tour just because it felt safer with him on the other side of the world. I haven't pursued anyone since then."

She was emotionally distant throughout the entirety of her story, and I felt my color draining as she went on. Once she finished, anger replaced the shock, and my hands clenched into fists. I wanted to find this man and beat him to a pulp. I wanted to ruin his life and take revenge for Nicole.

"I'm sorry, Sergeant I'm so sorry we failed you," I apologized, barely keeping my voice even, and the waitress brought our food.

Nicole shrugged and met my eyes. She didn't look angry or sad after telling her story. She just looked numb.

"You didn't fail me. You didn't create this system, and I doubt you could do anything to change it. I was continents away and a hell of a lot more naïve. I let that man control my life for over six months in Afghanistan and then another year and a half after that in my head.

I think I'm finally ready to stop letting him keep me from enjoying the present."

In my head, I acknowledged the potential cue to pry more information out of her about her interests in the opposite sex, but I couldn't bring myself to do it. After that story, I couldn't imagine coming clean about my feelings. It didn't change the way I felt about her at all, but the emotions felt so raw right now after talking about it that I felt like time was an appropriate buffer between now and my confession.

Instead, I moved the subject to something lighter, like our upcoming conference across the country as we ate. I would need her support to take my meetings' minutes and to manage correspondences as most of the big names would be flying in for it.

Reverting to work discussion seemed to improve her mood a little bit, but the flirty demeanor was gone. I didn't end up drinking any beer, but Nicole did, so I dropped her off at home before heading back to work. Instead of going into the office, though, I went to the gym to do some sparring with the equipment to blow off steam.

If I ever found out who did that to her, he would regret his existence.

10

Sergeant Massey

Colonel Lang's voice came through the receiver, "Sergeant, isn't this a pleasant surprise on a Saturday?"

"Colonel," I greeted him, grunting as I smacked the end of the wrench, loosening the nut just enough to break the calcium buildup sealing it. "I need a favor."

He was silent for a moment. "What do you need? Is everything okay?"

"Yeah, it's fine. I'm just doing some impromptu plumbing. Do you have a five-sixteenth-inches socket? I usually would, but it appears to be the only piece in the whole set to not have survived the move. I went to the store to buy a new one, but the store owner is running a scam, I swear. You're not allowed to buy a single socket; you must buy the whole set. I can order one online or drive to the next town over, but I'd rather not let this pipe leak any longer. I'm running out of towels."

"Sure thing, I'll be over in ten. Just a five-sixteenth?"

"Yep, that'll do it. See you soon."

I hung up and finished loosening up the nut connecting the two pipes. I decided to take a break, mostly so I could fix up my appearance. I looked like a bit of a train wreck at the moment. My hair was in a messy bun on top of my head, and I was wearing loose-fitting pajama shorts and a baggy T-shirt.

I changed into my old mechanic's uniform and a white, tight-fitting T-shirt. The onesie's top was rolled down, the arms tied around my waist. I always found myself strangely sexy in it, and I felt the need to pull out all the stops.

I took my hair out of the bun and brushed it back into a sleek ponytail, so the waves fell down my back. I added a touch of mascara and gloss to my lips before my time was up.

I hadn't planned on getting all prettied up today, or seeing Mr. Salt-and-pepper, but since he was coming over now, I figured I'd make the most of it. Even if he only stayed just long enough to drop off the socket.

Our lunch yesterday didn't quite go as planned. I wasn't planning on ever telling Riley about my ex-boyfriend, but he was persistent, and I thought it was fair he knew what baggage I had been carrying. He was calm throughout my story, but I could see the rage brewing in his eyes. It made me feel protected for a moment, and that was a feeling I hadn't had with a man for a long time. It also gave me a strange feeling of closure. I had spent so long being mad at myself that it was a relief to finally have someone else be angry for me.

I wanted to make it up to him. Even if it was a reaction he couldn't control, his response to things made me feel the desire to open up more. To share the pieces of myself that had been locked away for so long.

I had closed myself off for the better part of the past two years, and it was the first time I had really spoken about any of this. I wanted him to feel comfortable around me as well. I wanted him to open up to me. I wanted to be the person he divulged all the details of his life to, the one he lay with until the late hours of the night and whispered sweet nothings to.

I realized my thoughts were deviating from my promise to keep things casual and purely physical, and I quickly shut down those thoughts just as a knock sounded on the door.

I opened the door, and any mental preparation I had scrounged up prior to his arrival disappeared completely. He was wearing his tight white T-shirt and a pair of jeans and work boots. He was carrying a tool kit and a backpack, and it was the beginning of my fantasy.

I didn't say anything for a moment as I recovered but simply stepped out of the way and motioned for him to come inside. He looked around as he entered, his eyes scanning my place. I let out a silent sigh of relief that I had gone on a cleaning spree recently, so the place actually looked decent. He responded with an approving nod, and it made my heart thump.

"So, where's the damage?"

"The bathroom. This way." I led the way down the hall, turning back towards him. "Landlord is out of town this week, so I figured it was easier if I just fix it myself before he gets back. Besides, it was making quite a mess that I don't think could wait until he returned."

We stopped in front of the bathroom, and he let out a low whistle. The floor was caked with a thick layer of glistening towels. I sighed and grabbed a few more out of the closet and tossed them on the mess.

"Most of this was done by the time I woke up this morning. I shut off the water as soon as I could, but the residual water left in the pipes has an agenda still."

He pulled some extra towels out of his backpack, and we began clearing out the soaking ones and securing ourselves a dry path to the sink. We got on our hands and knees and crawled under the sink to assess the damage.

"You can see the middle pipe there has a network of hairline fractures through the PVC. I bought a new one to replace it, but that annoying ass bracket keeping it attached to the wall is being held by two five-sixteenth" bolts. That's where you come in, Coach…er…I mean sir."

My lip twitched, and we locked eyes. I then noticed how close we were. Our shoulders were practically touching, and the rest of our bodies were inches apart. Including our faces.

My eyes flickered down to his lips and the way he was looking at me made me wonder if he was thinking the same thing. I bit down on my lip, tempting him, and I could see the resolve wavering in his eyes. The sink made a hissing noise, and water sprayed out at us, ruining the moment.

"Okay, so I may have been lazy with turning off the water, but there were spiders, and I hoped I could fix it quickly."

Water dripped from our faces and the colonel chuckled, shaking his head. "I'll go get the water valve. You get the pipe ready to go."

He left me, and I riffled through his toolkit for the piece I needed. I quickly loosened the bolts and removed the bracket. I heard a hissing in the pipes and braced myself, but it only dripped out a little. He must have shut it off.

I replaced the pipe and was finishing up locking the bolts when he returned. I pushed myself out from under the sink, and he was standing right above me in the doorway. I smiled up at him, my clothes still soaked from the spray. He smiled and held out his hand, and I let him pull me up onto my feet. Then, I noticed we were both soaked from lying on the floor.

His shirt and jeans clung to him like a second skin, molding to his muscles in a way that wanted to bring me to my knees. I wanted to trace him with my fingers and tongue.

My eyes went back to his, and I saw the same hunger there. I glanced down to find my clothes sticking to me as well, my shirt leaving nothing to the imagination in its soaked state.

He stepped towards me until I was pressed against the sink and there were mere inches between us. I stared up at him with wide eyes, my lips parted and trembling.

"Your mascara is dripping," he told me, reaching out and wiping my cheek.

My sudden self-consciousness overcame my arousal and I quickly turned around, reaching for a cleansing wipe. *Cursed makeup. I never should have bothered.*

He stepped back to give me space while I cleaned myself up. I glanced up at him in the mirror and frowned. He looked ready to make up an excuse for leaving, but I realized I didn't want him to go.

"Hey, Colonel, I owe you for your help today. I have some beers in the fridge, and I wouldn't mind ordering a pizza. I can dry your clothes while we wait."

He looked up at me in surprise and relief. I misread him. He was looking for a reason to stay.

"Well, I can't say no to pizza and beer. I don't really have a change of clothes, though."

Though my mind went to a completely different place, my mouth managed, "It's all right. I have your T-shirt still if that'll help."

His lip twitched as if he was hoping I would dare to suggest something else. He followed me back to my room, standing in the doorway, while I dug out his shirt. I tossed it to him, and he immediately started stripping out of his clothes.

I grew flushed as I saw the hard muscles of his stomach but turned away out of embarrassment. I heard him mention something about meeting me in the living room, and he disappeared.

I quickly stripped out of my clothes into loose-fitting pajama shorts and a tank top. I took my hair down and shook it out over my shoulders. When I walked into the living room, I stumbled and stared. He was standing at the front window in a T-shirt and boxer briefs. I admired him for a moment before he turned toward me. His eyes gave me an appraising look, and he smiled.

"Your apartment is nice," he noted, walking over to me. He stood in front of me and handed me a phone. "I'm not sure what kind of pizza you like, but I prefer lots of meat."

"Meat lover's it is," I interrupted, smiling at him, and dialed the pizza place.

I probably should have tried to make it look like I didn't have the number memorized, but once I realized my mistake, I just decided to disappear to the kitchen to grab us a couple of drinks. I handed him one and fell on the couch. He sat down next to me and took a long drag from the can.

The silence created a barrier between us as we drank. I tried to find words to break it, but I couldn't scrounge up any until after I had finished my first beer. I grabbed us two more and sat a little more comfortably, my knee brushing the side of his leg.

"Listen, about the other day, what I said was a little intense. It hurt me a lot—what happened—but I shouldn't have written off all men. The risk seemed worth the reward back then, but now," —I looked up at him and met his eyes— "I'm not really sure."

His eyes flickered to my lips, and he reached his hand out to cradle my face as I leaned towards him. I wanted to kiss him. I needed it.

He leaned towards me, but before his lips met mine, the doorbell rang. I sighed as I stared into his eyes. We were inches away. I thought about making the pizza man wait, but then Riley pulled back.

I grabbed my wallet and went to the door, but Riley came up behind me and stuffed money in the pizza man's hand. I couldn't see how much it was, but it was way more than it should have been. I turned to protest, but he just grabbed the pizza and slammed the door. He set the pizza on the side table roughly and then pinned me against the door. He cradled my face and tilted my head back.

My shock only lasted for a moment as his lips pressed into mine. They were soft and warm and pliant against mine. After I recovered, I sighed against his lips, leaning into him. My fingers twisted into his hair as I opened myself up to him.

I thought the kiss might help to quell the passion growing inside me, but it made it unbearable. I wanted him. I needed him now. When my lips parted in my sigh, he deepened the kiss, and when my tongue ran along his bottom lip, his ran along mine soft as velvet.

I let out soft moans as his hands released mine to explore the rest of my body. His fingers brushed over my breasts, and my nipples strained against the thin fabric of my shirt. His thumbs caressed the sensitive buds, and I arched my back, gasping as molten pleasure sluiced through me. His knee slid between my legs, and I ground against him. My core was throbbing with need.

Deciding there were too many layers between us, I pulled off his T-shirt and tossed it on the ground. This encouraged him as he pressed his hips into mine and hitched up my thighs. I felt his erection through his boxers, and I wrapped my legs around his waist.

My hands ran down his bare chest, over the smooth muscles, until they found the hem of his boxers. I started to push them down, but he grabbed my hands and pinned them above me. I struggled against his grip, desperate to remove our remaining clothing so that I could have him inside me, but he held me tight.

"Slow down," he whispered against my lips.

He pressed his forehead against my shoulder, as if to catch his breath. My brain was fuzzy in its lust for him. I drew in a deep breath to clear my head a little once his lips weren't pressed against mine. I pressed my head back against the cool door.

"I'm sorry," I said breathily, and he looked up at me.

"Don't be sorry. I really want to—oh god, how I want to—I just want to wait until you're sober."

"I'm not—" I started, and then, I realized how fuzzy the world was. "Oh."

He grinned and pressed his forehead against mine and then leaned in and kissed me in a long, slow kiss before setting me on my feet. "When was the last time you ate?"

I gnawed on my bottom lip as I thought. "Uh…I had coffee this morning."

He frowned and reached for the box of pizza and handed it to me. "You need to take care of yourself. Eat."

I led us into the living room and set the pizza on the coffee table. We both grabbed a slice before sitting back on the couch. This time, he sat with his side pressed against me and his arm around my shoulder. It was such a simple gesture of affection that made me feel incredibly warm on the inside. This was not the feelings of someone wanting a low-risk, friends-with-benefits relationship with my superior. I was digging myself in far deeper than I would be able to pull myself out of.

11

Sergeant Massey

I wish I could say my weekend after consisted of hours of mind-blowing sex, but instead, we sat on the couch talking for the rest of Saturday. On Sunday, he spent the day preparing for a big meeting on Friday. Conversation flowed easily after we finally broke through the bubble of sexual tension that had been brewing and we texted a bit throughout the week.

We discussed some of our likes and dislikes, both in general and sexually. I told him about how my ex had the very traditional view about how men alone should be enough to please a woman and how because of it, I never had a chance to integrate toys into sex like I've wanted to. He seemed very interested in that. He found it incredibly arousing the subtle ways I teased him in the office and how it always made him want to bend me over the desk and just fuck me there.

I kept that in mind throughout the week, when I went against regulations and left a few of my top buttons unbuttoned.

Less subtly, I'd find any reason to drop stuff onto the floor and unnecessarily reach for a document or lean over his desk while he was on the phone to "borrow" a pen, giving him a full view of my cleavage. Even through his uniform, I could see the hardening of his shaft and, I wanted nothing more than to straddle him and sheathe him deep inside me.

On Thursday, it rained; however, poured was a more accurate term. I had forgotten my umbrella, so I got soaked in the five-minute walk from my car to the building. My clothes clung to me like a second skin, and my hair dripped as I set my purse on the desk. Riley was on the phone when I walked in, but now, there was silence.

I glanced over towards him and saw him watching me, his eyes dark and wanting. He mumbled something into the phone and hung it up before standing and walking towards me. He tilted my head back and kissed me chastely. I was surprised by his boldness, kissing me in the office. I sighed against his lips and leaned into him. When he pulled away, the front of him was damp. I smiled as I straightened out his clothes.

"I have a meeting to go to, but tomorrow, you're mine," he growled in my ear and made my knees weak.

He brushed his lips over mine and left. I was left in unwavering anticipation at the thought of what he planned for tomorrow. Perhaps, we would be taking a half day after his big meeting and he would take me back to his place and we would finally get the closure we needed. The thought kept me wet all day.

That night, I had a thorough prepping session. It had been a long while since I had been sexually active, and I needed the confidence boost, so I did a full-body lotion and pampering. It felt like it had been too long since I had treated myself like this, and come Friday morning, I was energetic and rejuvenated and ready for anything.

When I walked into the office, Riley was waiting for me in his best uniform. He looked hot, but my eyes were distracted by the small box in his hand.

"Sergeant," he greeted me gruffly, holding out the box. "The instructions are in the box. Please go to the bathroom and open it."

I stared at him in complete confusion, but he made no move to explain. Perhaps it was some sexy panties to wear under my uniform? He stared at me with an unreadable expression that unnerved me.

"Well, hurry up now, the meeting is starting soon, and I need you there to take notes."

"Yes, sir!" I quickly dashed out of the room to the bathroom. My cheeks grew dark red as I opened the box. *What am I supposed to do with this?*

I gulped as I held up the tiny vibrator. Just the thought of slipping it inside me made me slick.

I quickly reviewed the instructions: place this inside your pussy so that it rubs against your g-spot and leave it there until I tell you to remove it.

"What?" I said in a loud whisper.

My cheeks reddened before I hitched up my skirt and squatted, pushing it carefully inside me. I got it situated before pulling my skirt back down and circling my hips to get a feel for it. I could definitely feel it inside me and let out a little gasp of surprise as it rubbed against the sensitive spots. Moisture flooded between my legs, and I clamped them together. I let out a soft moan as every movement caused my legs to tremble. I didn't know if I would be able to make it to the meeting. I was getting aroused by the whole process, and it wasn't even turned on yet.

My phone chimed, letting me know I had a text message. I pulled it out and read the text and grimaced.

Is there a problem, Sergeant, it read. I rolled my eyes and quickly typed back. *No, sir.*

My phone chimed again. Then I'd appreciate some hustle. That's an order. Meeting in ten minutes. I will NOT be late!

I whimpered as I tried to adjust it to a position that didn't have me quivering. Fortunately, after walking around the bathroom a few times—mercifully, without interruption—I seemed to adjust to the foreign feeling, and though it sent tingles of pleasure soaring through me, my knees didn't threaten to give way with every step.

I made my way back to his office, and by the time, I closed the door behind me, I was red in the face and near panting. He had my notepad already in his hand and was ready to walk out the door as I walked in. He went to leave, but I put my hand up as I caught my breath.

"Don't worry, it's a short drive to the meeting. But if this is how you get after a little walk, I can't wait to see how you get when it vibrates."

"When it *what*," I yelped, but he had already walked out the door and down the hallway.

I hurried after him, but the friction was unbearable, so I slowed to a half waddle, half walk. Unfortunately, the meeting was in a room across campus, so we had to take the SUV over. I didn't get a chance to ask what he meant about the vibrations because the moment I was buckled in, it started.

I let out a soft noise of surprise as I arched up, my hand grasping the handle above the door. The buzzing grew more intense, and I couldn't help the series of mewls and whimpers that escaped my lips as I tried to maintain control.

"Whatever you do, Sergeant, do not come," he warned, and I glanced over at him with wanting eyes. I could come. I wanted to. I needed to.

As if he heard my thoughts, he shouted, "That's an order!"

"Yes, sir," I groaned as I resisted the desire and adjusted my position so the vibrator was pressed against a less sensitive spot inside me.

He took no mercy on me as he swerved through traffic on the base. He weaved almost violently, sending my whole body leaning from one side to the other and causing the vibrator to rub against different parts of me. Worse than this, though, was how he hit every bump and pothole in the road that jarred the vibrator deeper inside me and I thought I would come before we even reached the other building.

We finally made it to the venue, and he pulled into a spot, and the vibration disappeared.

I glanced over at him. His eyes were dark, and his knuckles were white as they gripped the stirring wheel. He leaned over towards me, and I tilted my head up towards him, expecting him to kiss me. He paused inches from my lips, and mine parted in anticipation. However, his hand reached past me and pulled the lever on the door, pushing it open.

"Come along, Sergeant Don't want to be late," he whispered.

His eyes shone with amusement, and he pulled away from me. I let out a shaky laugh in disbelief. He had me completely wrapped around his fingers.

As he got out of the car, I moved to follow him, letting out a muffled grown at how slick I was between my legs. This would be the longest meeting of my life. Before we entered the main hallway, where voices were carrying down, he paused and turned towards me.

"You'll sit behind me and take notes once the meeting's started. Don't come. Don't get up until the meeting is over and I stand up to leave. Understood?"

"Yes, sir," I responded in a meek voice, and he smiled before walking back towards the room.

His smugness riled me up, and a quip bubbled its way to my lips, but the vibrations started, and my lips slammed shut. We were some of the last to arrive at the conference room, which left me a moment in the hallway to compose myself before stalking in and finding an empty seat behind Riley.

Introductions were made first, and I struggled to keep my composure, as well as my voice, as normal as possible as I shook hands with those of higher rank than me.

Riley's eyes glinted with mischief as, partway through one of my sentences, he would increase the strength of the vibration and my voice would change pitches slightly.

Finally, they called for the meeting to start, and I quickly sat in the chair. Sitting didn't seem to help much though as it just kept the vibrator lodged deep inside me where my most sensitive areas were. He glanced back at me with a smirk on his face, and as the chairman started the meeting, I jumped when the buzzing started between my legs.

Nobody around me seemed to notice what was going on, but I clamped my thighs together as the vibrating increased for a moment before ebbing to a steady low vibration. Occasionally, the intensity oscillated, and my eyes rolled back as my grip tightened on my chair. I didn't bother trying to take notes. If Riley didn't take his own notes, he'd end up being shit out of luck.

I drew in a deep breath through my nose as the vibrations increased and bit my lip to suppress the noises threatening to break free. I shot daggers into the back of the colonel's head as he nonchalantly answered questions, completely unbothered by the way I was quivering behind him.

He glanced back at me a few times throughout the meeting, and desire and amusement flashed in his eyes. I could only catch a few words of the discussion before I was swooped back in.

I had shifted in my seat, and the vibrator was pressed firmly against my g-spot. I closed my eyes as they rolled back, and fortunately, the meeting ended soon after. I kept my composure as people trickled out of the room and kept myself mercifully quiet until it was just me and the colonel. He walked over to me and touched my arm.

"I'm sorry the meeting took so long. Let's go." He helped me out of my chair and steadied me as my legs shook. Once I could stand unaided, I retrieved my purse and glared at him. He leaned towards my ear and pressed his lips against me. "You look so hot right now. I'll make it up to you soon, I promise."

His words reignited the fire inside me.

12

Colonel Lang

I needed her home now. The meeting was torture. The vibrator I had given her had custom settings for the vibration, and I had set it to cycle through a variety of settings throughout the course of the meeting.

After she told me about her interests over text, I immediately set about ordering something to fit her needs. I spent a little extra on something that boasted complete discretion and completely customizable vibration settings.

I had more than earned my money's worth by the time we arrived at the conference building. The way she was panting and the noises she was making, her whole body tense and trembling, made my dick strain against my fatigues. I wondered if I should decline my attendance at the meeting and just take her home, but I liked the idea of her squirming throughout the meeting while she waited for me.

Once we arrived, I leaned toward her. I wanted to kiss her, but I knew if I did, I wouldn't be able to stop. Instead, I teased her, pushing the door open with a smug look on my face. In my pocket, I clicked a button on my remote and the vibration increased to maximum. The sassy comment I could see surfacing on her lips disappeared as her eyes rolled back.

I turned the setting down and got out of the vehicle. Her eyes were wild with fury and want and I couldn't wait to see that look later when she was pinned under me on the bed.

I couldn't wait to have her. She followed me inside, and each step looked like a struggle for her. I was surprised she had made it this far. I was half-hoping she would come on the ride over, but she was holding on.

The reviews promised a powerful and intense experience. She looked like she was about to go over the edge once I turned the vibrator on. I wondered if she would make it through the meeting.

I briefly considered making her come quickly and showing up a few minutes late. However, I had a feeling rumors would surface if I showed up late with a secretary who looked well sexed. It just wasn't professional. Me knowing there was a vibrator between her legs driving her wild was hardly professional either, but I was elated when she followed through with my orders to slip it inside her.

I couldn't help myself when she was having a conversation with one of our colleagues, and I played with the settings on the remote and watched her struggle to maintain the pitch of her voice. Sometimes, she slipped, and her words seemed rushed or high-pitched, and I grinned, pulling the attention of the officer to myself.

When the chairman called for the meeting to start, she gave me a hard glare before taking her seat. My fun was just beginning.

I glanced over at her several times to check on her and smiled. She was biting her bottom lip and gripping her pen so tightly I thought it would break. Her eyes were still sparked with fury and passion, and I wanted the meeting to just be over.

Ideally, everyone would have read the files I sent them, but I found myself and others reiterating information repeatedly to the generals. I resented them as every extra minute passed and every new, obvious question surfaced. By the end, I was barely able to suppress my glares as the conversation turned from professional to social. Didn't they realize some of us had places to be? I had months of sexual tension that I needed to work out tonight with the squirming, dripping woman sitting little more than five feet behind me.

Once the meeting was over, I turned back to her. Her eyes were closed, and sweat had beaded over her top lip and forehead. She was pale, and her body was shaking. I might have taken things a little too far.

I helped her onto her feet and watched her like a hawk the whole way to the car to make sure she stayed on her feet. I turned the vibration off completely while I drove home through traffic like a madman. Every time I veered too quickly, she moaned as she shifted in her seat. She was close, so close.

"Almost there, Sergeant," I told her, but she didn't respond.

When we finally pulled into the driveway of my house, I looked around to make sure we were alone before I kissed her. She moaned against my lips, and I reached into my pocket, turning the vibrator to full force.

I slid my hand up her thigh under her skirt and immediately felt wetness splattering her thighs. She spread her legs as I reached her panties which were soaked. I stroked her clit through the thin fabric.

She moaned against my touch and ground her mound against me. She was close to the breaking point; I could feel it.

"Come for me, Nicole," I whispered against her lips and she arched her back, crying out and digging her fingers into my hair.

The orgasm rocked through her violently, and she was left trembling and breathless. I kissed her forehead affectionately as I held her quivering body tightly. It took her a moment to come down, and she drew in long, deep breaths as she recovered.

Once her body relaxed, I fished the toy out from inside her pussy and she shuddered. She stared at me through lidded eyes and thick lashes with a lazy smile of pure satisfaction stretched across her face. I would get to see that smile many more times as I promised both of us that this wouldn't be the only time she came tonight.

"I want you upstairs, in my room, now," I demanded, and a defiant glint sparked in her eyes. "That's an order, Sergeant"

"Yes, sir," she slurred and sat up, kissing me chastely.

I needed her in the bedroom now. I quickly scurried out of the SUV and into the house. She followed sluggishly behind me, her legs still trembling slightly.

I made it to the bedroom first and was in the process of taking off my clothes when she walked in. She quickly helped me pull off my shirt and unbutton my pants before she admired me a moment. Slowly, I unbuttoned her blouse, my lips trailing behind my fingers, and once I had dropped it onto the floor, my eyes ran over her.

A soft blush spread over her face and neck, down to her breasts, as I had imagined. It was all as I imagined. I softly ran my thumbs over her nipples. She moaned and squirmed underneath me.

I groaned as I pressed my lips to hers and kissed her deeply and with such passion that I knew that, tonight, I would lose myself in her.

13

Sergeant Massey

Fortunately, the walk to the SUV was short. I worried I would not have been able to make it if the vehicle was farther away.

Once we got into the car, I hoped he would let me come right there, but he just commanded me to buckle up and took off. Once again, he took no mercies with me, and I was close to going mad from the way my body was being overloaded. I moaned without restraint as it was the only way I could release the built-up frustration. I tried lifting my butt off the seat, but when he hit a pothole, it sent the vibrator deeper inside me and threatened to push me over that blissful edge.

"Almost there, Sergeant," he assured me as I whimpered.

He took it a little easier on the driving, but it was near impossible to resist the need to come. I didn't want to find out what would happen if I did.

Finally, the car came to a stop outside his house and I leaned back, my breaths short and hurried. I was so close to coming.

He quickly unbuckled us both and pulled me closer to him. He kissed me and slid his hand up my skirt. Just the feeling of his fingers brushing against my inner thigh caused me to shiver. He mumbled against my lips something about how wet I was before he began to stroke my clit. My hips bucked, and my body began to tremble.

"Come for me, Nicole," he whispered against my lips, and with his permission finally came my release.

My muscles clamped down on the vibrator as it continued its assault and his fingers pressed harder against my swollen bud. My hands found their way up into his hair, and I cried out as pleasure tore through me blindingly.

It was the strongest orgasm I had had, and it rocked through my whole being. I needed this. I needed a release. The peak was overwhelming and took my breath away. When I was finally able to catch it, he pulled me tightly in his arms. I glanced up at him appreciatively with a drunken expression and bit my lip as I smiled. His eyes darkened, and he pulled the vibrator out of me.

"I want you upstairs, in my room, now," he demanded, and I raised my eyebrow at him. "That's an order, Sergeant"

"Yes, sir."

He raised an eyebrow in surprise when I submitted immediately rather than challenged him. I kissed him, and the moment I pulled away, he left the car and rushed towards the house. I was left in shock for a moment before I went after him. My legs were still shaking, so I was a bit slower, and by the time I reached the bedroom, he was in the midst of taking off his clothes.

I walked up to Riley and helped him unbutton the rest of his shirt before pulling it off him and running my hands up the firm muscles of his abdomen and over his chest. He tensed under my fingers, and I traced them back down. I unbuttoned his pants and pushed them to the ground. My heart skipped a beat as I stared at his mostly naked form. His body could have been sculpted by the Greeks. He was truly a work of art.

His hands grasped the front of my blouse as he pulled me into him and kissed me. I let out a soft moan against his mouth, and he began to unbutton my blouse as his lips trailed down my neck and then down farther between my breasts and over my stomach.

I arched my back as his hands ran up my body and pushed the blouse off my shoulders. My bra followed soon after, and he stepped back to admire me.

I felt vulnerable exposed like this, so my first reaction was to cross my arms over my chest. He shook his head and clicked his tongue against his teeth as he pulled me against him. His hands slowly ran down my stomach and unbuttoned my skirt before pushing it and my panties to the floor. I reached my hands up and held on to his shoulders for balance.

As his hands trailed their way back up my thighs, he hitched them up and laid me back on the bed gently and hovered over me. He pinned my arms above my head as his gaze ran over me.

"Let me appreciate you," he growled, and I reddened.

With his free hand, he brushed his fingers over my breast and his thumb over my nipple. I leaned into him as I gasped softly. I thought it would take me longer to get worked up right after I came, but my body was more than ready to go again.

I lifted my hips to grind against him and he pressed into me, allowing me to feel the full-mast erection between his legs. When he released my hands, I ran them down his chest and all the way down to cradle his shaft.

He sucked in a breath and groaned as I palmed him. He hovered above me a moment as he met my eyes. Both of us were wild with desire, our eyes mad with passion. I wanted him. I needed him. My fingers tightened around his hardness, and I felt it twitch.

"I can't wait any longer, Massey. I need to fuck you."

I whimpered, and he pushed his boxers off. He hung full erect at a size that both excited and scared me. He certainly had nothing to compensate for.

Riley leaned down and kissed me as he lined himself up at my entrance. I let out a soft sigh against his lips as he rubbed the thick head of his cock against me and pressed into my clit. He lifted himself just far enough that he could see my face as he guided his head inside me.

Slowly, he thrust the rest of his length deep within me, and I winced at the sharp pain caused from his size. He paused for a moment when he was seated within me so I could get used to him. I had never been so stretched or felt so full. I clenched my muscles down around his thickness, and he groaned and started to pull out of me. The friction of his shaft rubbing against my walls made me shiver.

He leaned back down to kiss me as he began to pump in and out of me, picking up speed until he found a steady rhythm—fast and hard. His tongue stroked mine, and I moaned against his lips as the familiar knot stirred in my lower abdomen. Every time he thrust into me, I felt myself getting closer to the edge, and my breath picked up as I gripped onto him tighter.

"Come for me, Nicole."

His words struck me like a jolt of electricity that concentrated right on my core. His tone was deep and sensual. I let out a soft cry against his ear as his dick rubbed against my g-spot and nearly pushed me over the edge.

"Come with me," he begged, and with three more thrusts, he stopped with his shaft deep inside me.

My fingers twisted into the pillow above me as I lifted my hips off the bed and rocked against him. Pleasure washed over me like a tidal wave, and I cried out. His dick spasmed, and a warm liquid spurted inside me.

I let out a low noise as I came down, twitching along with his dick, as he finished. Finally, he collapsed on top of me with his head against my neck. His breath was hot against my skin as we recovered.

Once we had our breaths, he kissed me softly before pulling out of me and getting up. He grabbed a towel and wiped up between my legs before grabbing my hand.

"Come shower with me."

Without waiting for an answer, he pulled me up onto my feet. I stumbled, and he held me up against him. I groaned as I would have loved to take a nap and snuggle against him instead.

Sleepily, I leaned against the sink while he got the shower ready. I stepped in and stood under the hot stream of water, sighing as it relaxed my body even further.

Riley got in behind me, and I closed my eyes as he pressed up against my back. His muscular frame felt wonderful. I opened my eyes when I felt a warm washcloth against my arm. The colonel was washing me. He was gentle as he brushed the cloth over my body, and I leaned my head back against him as he explored every inch. I gasped when he pushed a finger inside my sex and gently stroked my walls.

"Washing you out for later." He hummed against me, and I sighed pleasantly.

He removed his hand, and I couldn't hold back a whimper. I turned towards him, and he was grinning. I grabbed the washcloth and began to wipe him down, carefully switching places under the stream. I took extra care of his nether regions, and once we were satisfied, he shut off the water and handed me a towel.

I dried myself off and wrapped the towel around me and then watched him dry himself off and toss the towel into the laundry before walking out of the room naked. I couldn't help myself but to admire the view.

"Come on, Massey, let's eat," he called over his shoulder, and I gave him a look.

Back to calling me by my last name. What was this to him, really? A small part of me was hurt at the thought he might consider this just sex, but I quickly quelled that voice. It was safer that way.

14

Sergeant Massey

I couldn't decide whether to go downstairs naked or wrapped in a towel. It required a boost of confidence I should've had following the most incredible sex we just had, but the voice in the back of my head warned against it. I wished I had thought to bring a change of clothes. Maybe I could find one of his T-shirts and wear that around.

"Sometime today, Massey," he called upstairs, and I huffed. "Drop the towel and move it. That's an order."

I cursed him and the way my body grew warm whenever he ordered me around. I debated slipping into my work clothes and running home, but they had been through a lot today and desperately needed a wash. He drove me here, so I would have to walk. *Ugh! Why did I have to live so damn far away?*

I took a deep breath, and without looking into the mirror, I took the towel and dropped it into the laundry bin.

Walking around his house naked should have felt odd, yet this scenario had played in my head so many times it felt natural. When I got to the kitchen, he was standing at the counter with a frying pan and a handful of ingredients. He was completely naked, and from my position, I got a great view of his backside. I let out a low, flirtatious whistle, and I could see a smile forming on his lips.

"What do you want in your omelet?" he asked without looking away from the cutting board.

I eyed the ingredients he had sitting on the counter. "Bell peppers, mushrooms, and cheese." I watched him as he moved around his kitchen. I wanted to approach so many subjects. What were we? What did he expect from me?

Anxiety set in, and I wondered what he thought of me. Did he think I was easy? Did he have a thing for younger women? Was I special?

"And before you ask, no, I don't usually sleep with those in my command. You're the first." I jerked at his words and met his eyes. The way he did that was uncanny, and I narrowed my eyes at him before he added, "You had that look in your eyes. I could see the questions brewing at the surface and then came the anxiety."

I hated being so transparent, but I also appreciated that he could sense my nervousness and immediately sought to reassure me. I lifted my jaw as I tried to brush it off. I didn't want him to think of me as young and insecure.

"Really? Well, I don't usually sleep with my superiors, either." He smirked at me and turned back towards the food. I felt like I needed to get more questions off my chest, so I walked up behind him and began to trace my fingers over his back. "How long has it been since, uh, you know?"

"Two years since I had been with anyone."

I was surprised at this fact. He was very attractive and wouldn't have any issue getting a woman of any age. I nodded my head and began to rub his muscles. He let out a deep, appreciative sigh.

"So, why me? What makes me so special?"

"I'm not so sure. The moment I first saw you, I was drawn to you. It was odd for me, as I hadn't been attracted to anyone so young. A few years younger than me at most, no more than five or six, but with you, it was irresistible."

He turned towards me and rubbed his hands up my arms before tilting my head back. He kissed me, and I leaned into him. He pulled away to flip the omelet and smiled at me. "This is definitely something special."

I felt warm on the inside and childishly giddy. He handed me the omelet, and I leaned against the counter as I dug in. It was delicious. I moaned, and he gave me a dark look.

"You know, I was mostly surprised that you were single. You asked about my relationship issues but never came forward about your own. How the hell are you still single?"

I could see the tension rising in his back, and I worried I might have crossed a line.

"I was married, once, years ago, but it didn't end up working out. I cared about her, but my true love back then was work. She couldn't handle the military wife life, and so, she left me for someone who wasn't gone all the time. I don't really blame her. It was easy to stop missing her.

"I stayed single for a few years out of respect for her, but then I decided to start dating again. By that time, most of the women my age were already married or not interested in anything serious.

"I didn't think I'd enjoy casual sex, but then, I matured and found it was a lot easier in this line of work. I enjoyed the flings but never really found anyone I was interested in having anything serious with." He glanced over at me, and I paused at his serious expression. "Well, that is, until now."

He turned away, and my heart skipped a beat. My eyes stung a moment, and I pushed the omelet around on the plate. It was the first moment I finally acknowledged I had deep feelings for the colonel that I couldn't push back. I would get myself burned, for sure, but it felt good and I didn't want to let that go.

"Finish your breakfast, Nicole. That's an order."

I raised an eyebrow at him and snorted. He stared me down and I caved, putting another bite in my mouth.

He laughed, sliding his omelet onto his plate. "Say whatever you want. I see your attempts at disobedience, but you always submit in the end."

"No, I don't," I huffed, and he leaned towards me with a smirk.

"Yeah, you do. But it's all right. I find it cute."

I playfully objected, and our banter continued throughout the rest of breakfast. It had been a while since I'd felt this comfortable with anyone. Even if I got burned, I was going to enjoy it. I had spent years exercising control and I was ready to finally let go a little.

Once breakfast was done, he cleared off the dishes and ordered me to sit on the table. I narrowed my eyes at him but obeyed, much to my chagrin. His eyes were hungry as he approached me. I spread my legs in anticipation as his cock was at full mast. I was surprised. He certainly had the most stamina of any of the men I'd ever been with. He pinned my hands behind my back with one hand as he stared into my eyes.

"Be mine, Nicole. Submit to me," he begged and ran his free hand down an arm. I shuddered at his touch.

"Isn't that what I have been doing?"

He leaned down and kissed my nipples with quick pecks before running his lips down to my stomach. I sucked in a breath, anticipating him going farther.

He stood up, looked me in the eyes, and then shook his head. "Not completely, not without second-guessing. Stop pausing, stop thinking, just be with me."

He leaned forward and kissed my lips softly. His fingers brushed over my inner thigh, and I gasped against his lips, flicking my tongue out against his.

"Trust me, Nicole. Stay with me, be with me. You won't regret a single moment; this I promise you."

He released my hands as he pulled away to give me space to think. I bit my lip as I mulled it over. If I didn't leave now, this would be something more than what I came here for. I would break my promise to myself.

"And if I say no?" I asked, and he moved farther away.

Hurt flashed in his eyes. "Then I will take you home and won't bother you about this ever again. We had a good time so far and I appreciate that time with you, but I have no interest in pressuring you into something you're not comfortable with. I want to pursue you. I want to continue this with you. But if you want to stop at any point, then I'll back off. I have no intention of taking advantage of you nor do I want you to think that I would jeopardize our professional relationship."

It wasn't easy being this close to him. I propped myself up on my elbows. He seemed genuine with his words. We were both at our most vulnerable like this, and he was giving me the assurances I was most looking for. He understood my position and promised not to take advantage. My resolve wavered, and I made my decision. I met his eyes and nodded.

"Say it, please." His eyes held such an intensity that it took my breath away.

"Yes, I will be yours."

Riley grinned at me before leaning down to kiss me. He slowly pushed me back until he pinned me against the table. The passion in his kiss was overwhelming. He left me breathless as he moved to kneel down between my legs. I bit my lip and moaned as his lips ran along my inner thigh. His hands held my legs spread, and he placed gentle kisses around my mound and then stroked my sensitive bud with his tongue.

I gasped as he spread me open and traced the tip of his tongue over my nether lips. He teased my entrance before swirling around my clit. He didn't let up until he had me writhing and screaming for him not to stop. My fingers held him against me as I ground my core against his mouth until I came.

He didn't give me a moment to recover before standing up and pushing himself into me. I cried out in ecstasy. I hadn't come this much ever. I worried he would shatter my mind as I felt another orgasm building. He grabbed my hips and rocked me against him, and the orgasm that followed was more intense than the last.

"God, you're so tight," he groaned before shooting his seed deep inside me. He pulled me up to kiss me softly and stared into my eyes as we caught our breaths. "That was intense."

I nodded, unable to manage words. He kissed my lips softly before pulling out and stepped away from me.

"Come on, let's rinse off and get dressed. I'll drive you back to your place so you can pack an overnight bag, and then, we'll go out to eat somewhere."

I stared at him in disbelief. How could he still have the energy to do anything? I was ready to sleep for the rest of today and well into tomorrow. I questioned my ability to walk after taking his well-endowed cock twice today. However, my stomach rumbled, and I was surprised. How was I still hungry?

"Well, food does sound pretty good right now... I feel famished," I admitted, and he smiled.

"Seemed to have worked up an appetite...of sorts."

I blushed as he ran his eyes over me, and I grew both afraid and excited at the idea of going again. However, he backed away and turned towards the door.

"Come on, Sergeant" He glanced back at me briefly before disappearing up the stairs.

15

Colonel Lang

It took everything in me not to beg. When I asked her to be mine, the hesitation in her eyes hurt even though I understood it. I hadn't intended on asking her to be exclusive with me, to be with me, but after being so intimate with her, after seeing her so vulnerable and entirely mine, I realized I wanted more. So, I asked her. I couldn't resist.

In her eyes, I saw reluctance but also a desire to say yes. She wanted me, as I wanted her, but after being hurt in the past, the wall wasn't going to be knocked down so easily. I sweetened the deal, targeted the anxieties I knew we were both having and could see her giving it legitimate thought. Then she nodded. but I knew I needed to hear those words.

"Say it, please," I told her, and she stared into my eyes.

"Yes, I will be yours."

I grinned as I leaned down and kissed her. Mine. She was mine. I pinned her wrists behind her as I captured her lips. I needed her. I needed to taste her. I got onto my knees and held her legs spread.

As I kissed her thighs, I heard her sigh. Every noise she made drove me wild. I kissed my way to the apex between her thighs and stroked my tongue over her. She moaned and squirmed. I parted her lips and really tasted her. I grabbed her thighs and pulled her closer to my mouth as I flicked my tongue around her clit, enjoying every gasp and whimper she made.

I could feel her getting closer as her muscles spasmed against me and fluid flooded into my mouth. I lapped at her, and she shook in my grip as she came. My dick was throbbing and in desperate need of her pussy, so I waited until she was staring down at me with those dreamy eyes before I stood up and I sheathed myself in her.

She grabbed onto the edge of the table as she thrust her hips in tandem with mine. I held back the need to come immediately. Seeing her like this made it so easy, but I wanted her to come with me again.

I felt her muscles clamping down on me, and I tensed up. She was so tight around me. My dick throbbed, and I came, shooting my load deep inside her. I pulled her up to be pressed against my chest and kissed her. I wanted to carry her up to the bedroom and lie with her for hours, but I knew an omelet wouldn't cover all the energy we had lost and would lose. I hadn't thought to make a grocery list this week, though, so it was all I had. Plus, she needed stuff for the weekend.

Despite my reservations, I pulled out of her and turned towards the stairs. "Come on, let's get dressed. I'll drive you back to your place so you can pack an overnight bag, and then, we'll go out to eat somewhere."

I noted my legs were a bit sore. It had been a while since I'd used these muscles, and I was paying for my two-year break now. I knew I should probably take it slow, but I had been waiting over two months to have her and now that I could, I was going to relish every second with her.

She was moving slowly when following me up the stairs, and I could tell she was sore as well. It brought me a swell of pride to know I could do that to her.

I admired her while she dressed and watched her blush when her eyes met mine. She didn't bother with underwear as hers were soaked, and it made my cock stir to know she wasn't wearing any. I knew if I tried to go again, though, there was no way either of us would be able to walk afterward. But hell, if it wasn't tempting…

We pulled up outside her place, and she glanced at me. "So, what do I need for this weekend?"

"Well, really just a toothbrush, but it's up to your discretion." She deadpanned, and I chuckled. "I would like you to stay the rest of the weekend. So, bring workout clothes, day clothes, and work clothes for Monday. I mean, you might want to change your clothes right now, too, but if you want to keep the underwear off, that's also fine with me."

I grinned as she blushed and quickly hopped out of the car. I leaned back in my seat as I watched her go with a satisfied smile on my lips. She was mine. Maybe it wouldn't last, maybe we'd break up in the end, but for now, she was mine.

I was still smiling to myself when she returned with a duffel bag. She was wearing a pair of leggings and a tank top, and I half-hoped she would drop her bag and show me a view of her ass before she got into the car.

"What are you smiling about?" She narrowed her eyes, and I reached out, tilting her chin and swiping my thumb along her bottom lip.

The suspicion dissolved from her face as her eyes softened and her lips parted. She was so beautiful. I didn't answer her question as I turned back to the wheel and started driving. "There's a diner just outside of town that has *the best* apple pie I've ever had. Mind going there?"

"I'll defer to your judgment, sir." She smirked as she buckled in and looked off into the distance.

I let the silence linger and just appreciated her presence at this moment. Once we were seated in the diner, I watched her with admiring eyes. I had done a quick scan to make sure I didn't recognize anyone, but the only one I knew was our waitress. She had a curious look in her eyes as it was the first time she'd seen me with a woman, but she didn't make any comment. Nicole was looking at the menu with complete concentration, and so, I had a few moments to trace my gaze over her features. I wanted to know everything about her. I wanted to know her hopes and dreams and her desires in life.

"So, Nicole," I started, and she glanced up at me.

She must have been surprised at the seriousness in my eyes and tone as she quickly put down the menu and gave me her full attention. "Yes, s-sir. I mean, uh, Riley?" She tested my name for the first time, and I smiled.

"Tell me more about yourself." I reached my hand out and placed it over her hand, stroking my thumb over the back of her hand.

Her eyes widened in surprise. "What do you want to know?"

The questions were endless, but I filtered for the best to start with—the one that circled around in my head the most: the future.

"Your enlistment ends in just over nine months. What are you plans after it's over?"

She bit her lip as she thought before speaking. "You know, that's a question I've been asking myself for a while now. I had thought I would be career military like my dad, so I didn't consider what I wanted to do with the rest of my life.

"Now, I'm ready to be out, and I have no real plans. I'd like to start living my father's dream for me again, if I could. I know the military will pay for school, plus I have a quite a bit in my savings to last me for a while.

"I'm a different woman than I was when I graduated high school, so I'd like to try to go back to college. What kind of degree I'd pursue, though, that's the real question. I'd like to do something that would allow me to help and support people as they work towards their goals and fight prejudices. Maybe, something in human resources, or maybe, I'd like to be a counselor. It'd be nice to be in a position where I can challenge existing hierarchies and help pave the way and provide resources for women in the future to rise to the top."

She was so genuine and pure it made my heart ache. She met my eyes, blushed, and then diverted her gaze back down at her hands.

"That's noble. I admire you for that."

She glanced up at me and smiled. "What about you? Did you picture yourself being a career military man? Or what did you want to do?"

"Er, no. When I graduated high school, I didn't really have a plan or a purpose, but I needed to do something, so I enlisted with some friends. Turns out, I'd found what I was good at, and I grew to like it.

"We all rose fairly quickly in the ranks and ended up stationed in the Middle East doing classified government missions. We were pretty damn good at what we did and were reaching the end of our time served when we had a mission that went awry. We all got sent home: me and two caskets." The color drained from her face, and she squeezed my hand.

"I'm so sorry, Riley. I saw the picture on your fridge. Was that you and your friends?"

"Yeah, me, Andrew, and Seymour. Andrew had a pregnant girlfriend he was planning to propose to once we finished this mission. Seymour was planning on settling back down in our hometown and starting his own construction business with his dad.

"Instead of following their dreams, they got funerals. I got a medal and a promotion and a desk job at the base. I was kind of lost without the military. This was all I really knew and didn't know what to do if I left, so I stayed in.

"It's been twenty-two years and it's still all I can picture myself doing. One day, I'll retire, but I don't know when that will be. I don't do well with idle time, and it keeps me busy."

I didn't tell her when I stopped throwing myself into work my mind got caught in an endless loop of guilt that I was the one who made it home. I didn't tell her I often thought about what Seymour and Andrew would be doing if they were alive.

I also didn't tell her how I was the only one of the three of us who had no plan or future or direction in my life and how I constantly battled with myself that I was the one who shouldn't have made it home.

16

Sergeant Massey

My heart ached as I saw the pain surfacing in his eyes as he told his story. I wanted to hold him and never let go. I wished we had some semblance of privacy, but I was all too aware of the curious gazes of the waitress and the other patrons around us.

He finished his story, but I could feel words lingering in the air, unsaid. I squeezed his hand, and the waitress brought our food. We made idle small talk throughout, but I appreciated how he always seemed to respect the sacred silence of mealtimes to give me time to properly bond with my food.

The food gave me a temporary energy boost on the way home, as I was much livelier and more talkative, but when we walked through the door, exhaustion rolled over me in a tidal wave.

I swayed as I slowly pulled off my shoes, and he put his arm around me, and he led me upstairs. I hadn't been this drained in a while, but I enjoyed every second of it. I brushed my teeth in a daze before stripping and crawling into bed. Riley joined me soon after, sliding up behind me. He chuckled and commented how he appreciated how well trained I was when I immediately removed my clothes. I mumbled a retort, but with his comforting warmth stretched against me, I was quickly swept away to sleep.

I woke up the next morning feeling more well rested than I had in a while. I stretched out against the sheets and brushed against something that made me pause. I glanced around, and it took me a moment to remember I wasn't at home but had stayed over at Riley's house.

The events of yesterday replayed in my mind, and warmth glowed inside of me as I pulled the blankets tightly against me. I turned over to see Riley still sleeping beside me. He was stretched out on his back and only covered in a sheet that fell over his waist. I might have stolen the blankets, but that thought was fleeting as I noticed the slight tenting of the sheet at his waist. I blushed as I reached my hand out to cup his erection, and I wondered what kind of dream he was having.

I slowly pulled the sheet away to reveal his beautiful length before taking it in my hand again. I stroked him steadily before he shifted in his sleep. I admired it and wanted to know what he tasted like.

I moved down under the sheets between his legs and positioned myself over him. I kept one hand tightly around the base of his cock and leaned down and ran my tongue over the head, curiously. A small amount of precum wet the tip of his cock, and I licked it up as I pulled more of him into my mouth, wrapping my lips around the head.

I slid my mouth down his shaft, swirling my tongue around the head when I came up. He groaned in his sleep and shifted. I took as much of his dick into my mouth as I could before I felt it tickling my throat. There was no way I was going to fit his full length in my mouth, so I settled for using my hand and mouth to pump him.

He didn't wake as I continued to run my hand and lips up and down his shaft, picking up the pace as I went. His cock began to throb, and I knew he was close.

His thighs squeezed around me as he bucked his hips up, shoving his dick deeper into my mouth, spurting warm liquid down my throat.

I pulled back in surprise but managed to catch all his seed as he finished. I swallowed the last bit as I popped his dick out of my mouth, and he threw the sheets back over my head. I sat up on my knees and wiped my mouth before smiling at him. "Good morning, Riley."

He let out a breathy laugh before pulling me down next to him and pressing against me. "'Good morning, Riley' she says as she wipes my cum from the corner of her lips. Nicole, you'll drive a man crazy," he growled, and I grinned.

"Yes, sir!" I agreed, and he hummed as he kissed me.

"What a wonderful way to wake up," he murmured against my lips.

"Mmm, I'm glad you enjoyed it. Now, I think I'm ready to wake up with coffee and a long run."

He growled at my words, flipping me and pinning me underneath him with my back against his chest. He pulled my leg over his as he knelt behind me, spreading me open. He nuzzled my ear, neck, and shoulder as he ran his hands up my sides to cradle my breasts. He caressed his thumbs over my nipples, and I parted my legs farther and rubbed my ass against him. He flicked my nipples and teased them, and I moaned as I twisted my fingers into the sheets in front of me.

Once he had me squirming, he grew a little rougher, pinching and tugging, and I mewled as I ground myself into him. I felt his cock getting harder as he started to rock his hips against my backside.

He slipped a hand down between my legs and ran his fingers through my nether lips, finding me soaked and ready. He dipped a finger into me and stroked my insides a few times before bringing his finger out to rub my clit.

"You think you can just suck me off and run?" he whispered in my ear.

"No, sir," I said in a breathy voice. I honestly wasn't expecting him to reciprocate, but here he was, drawing lazy circles across the tip of my sensitive bud.

"You think I would let you go without returning the favor and letting you have your own release?"

"No-no, sir," I whimpered. I could feel the tightness building in my core. I would've been fine to let him come without asking for anything in return. I was sure he would get me later, but now that he had me, I would do anything for him not to stop.

He slipped his hardness inside me and moved in and out slowly, never moving his finger off my swollen bud. "Tell me, Sergeant, is this what you wanted?"

"Y-yes, sir," I moaned. Gods, yes, this was what I wanted.

"Or would you rather go for a run?" he said in a hoarse voice.

I let out a whimper as he stopped moving. "No, please, don't stop."

"Tell me what you want, Sergeant?"

"I want you to fuck me, sir."

"Good answer," he growled before picking up where he left off. He thrust inside me in long, tantalizing strokes.

I let out a shaky breath as my body shook underneath him. From this position, he was pushing even deeper inside me, his head rubbing against my g-spot perfectly. I let out a small cry as I felt the tension in my core building to a climax, and I shuddered as I was pushed over the edge.

He finished a moment after me, pressing his cock all the way in as it throbbed, and shot his load into me. I moaned and bit down on the pillow, squeezing him with my thighs as my muscles clamped hard around him. He bent down over me as we both came down and brushed his lips over my shoulder.

"Was that the wake-up you were looking for?" he murmured, and I chuckled breathlessly.

"Yes, sir."

"Good, let's get dressed and go for a run. Gotta get that workout in while you can still walk."

I turned and gave him a dark look, and he grinned. He got out of bed and stretched before pulling on gym shorts and a T-shirt. I slowly worked my muscles as I sat up in bed, rubbing my trembling thighs. He tossed me a towel, and I wiped up between my legs before making my way into the bathroom.

Starring at myself in the mirror, I looked relatively rejuvenated, considering the past twenty-four hours. My dark circles were almost nonexistent, and my bedhead looked more sexy than terrifying. I tamed my hair and pulled it back into a ponytail. I washed my face, cleaned myself up, and then walked back into the bedroom to grab my running clothes. He admired me from the doorway as I dressed.

"You like what you see?" I bit my lip and placed my hand on my hip, walking towards him.

"I'd like it better if you went running without clothes on."

I gave him a sly smile and raised my eyebrow as I walked past. "Oh yeah, are you going to visit me in prison since I'm sure I'll be arrested for indecent exposure and all?"

"Well, I'd write letters at least."

I let out a hearty laugh, and he pulled me into him. He kissed me chastely, leaving me breathless, before running down the stairs and out of the house. I let out a cry of surprise at the abruptness and chased after him.

17

Colonel Lang

The last twenty-four hours with Nicole had sparked a fire within her. Those walls that had been blocking her from my access crumbled more and more with every kiss and the defiance in her gaze had leaked into her words. She walked with an attitude, flirted shamelessly, and bit her lip with a sly smile after she made some lewd comment or innuendo. She was actually the match I expected her to be and the one I so long wanted to free.

If anyone expected our sex session to curb the overwhelming desire I had for her in any way, then they were dead wrong.

As we ran, I found myself hopelessly falling for her in ways that I never imagined. My heart tugged whenever she told me about her hopes and dreams and experiences, and genuine laughter bubbled out of my lips every time she teased me or made a generalized jab at all men. I wanted nothing more than to simultaneously fuck her raw and lie with her in bed bantering and wrapped in each other's arms.

As we neared the end of our several-mile run, I was impressed with her ability to keep up. I usually had a pretty quick pace comparatively, but she never lagged behind, and she even encouraged me to go an extra mile more than normal.

By the time we made it back home, she was slick with sweat but far from breathless. I handed her a bottle of water and a towel from the kitchen, and we leaned against the counter as we chatted.

She took a big sip from her bottle, and water dripped down her chin and disappeared down her neck, beneath the collar of her shirt. I paused in my drinking and set the bottle on the counter. I walked up to her, and she lowered her water bottle hesitantly. I tilted her head back and ran my tongue from the edge of her shirt, up the waterline on her neck, and stopped at the corner of her lips.

"Mmm, it tastes better this way."

Her eyes widened before growing dark and flirtatious. She bit her lip and pulled me down into a kiss. Her mouth was cold from the water, but her tongue seared mine.

"Upstairs. Shower. Now," I demanded, pulling away from her, and a disobedient flame ignited in her eyes, but instead of speaking her mind, she just stripped into nothing and walked past me. I admired both sides of her before following her.

I stripped as she got the shower ready, and I moved in after her. She picked up a cloth, but I snatched it before she could begin to wipe herself down. I gently began to scrub at her skin, and she leaned back into me, letting out a shaky breath as I sensually soaped her up. I ran my hands down her front and between her legs. She drew in a sharp breath as I rested my palm over her mound.

"Are you sore?" I asked, teasing my fingers through the soft hair above her nether lips.

"No, sir." Her voice shook, and she ground her hips lightly against me.

I slipped a finger inside her, stroking in and around her sex with one hand, while running my other hand down her back and in between her ass cheeks, teasing her rosebud. She let out a soft cry of surprise but made no noise of protest, but I paused anyway.

"Relax. I want you to enjoy this. If you feel any pain or discomfort, tell me, and I will stop. I would never try to force you into anything or do anything to hurt you."

She nodded her head, but she was still tense, so I pressed against her rosebud lightly but didn't enter and continued to pump my other finger inside her tight pussy.

Once she relaxed a little, I pushed my finger past her rosebud until it was in knuckle-deep. She tensed again but then adjusted to the feeling and began to rock her hips against my hands. She seemed to be enjoying both sensations, and I pushed my finger in a little farther, and she moaned.

"How does that feel?"

"Wonderful, please don't stop," she whispered breathlessly, and I grinned.

I began to pick up my pace, and I felt her beginning to unravel against me. I pumped my fingers in and out of both of her holes, and she whimpered as she shuddered against me. Her dripping core and tight anal passage began to clench down on my fingers as she grabbed my arm. Her legs shook and her body trembled, and within seconds, she was moaning long and hard as an orgasm ripped through her. I popped my fingers out of her holes and washed them off in the warm water.

"Are you ready for number three?" I asked as she came down.

I shut off the water and grabbed a towel, drying us off before picking her up and carrying her to the bed. I placed her on her back with her ass on the edge of the bed, lifted her legs over my shoulders, and sheathed myself into her, thrusting fast and hard.

She moaned in pleasure as she begged me to keep going. I told her to rub her clit as I held onto her tightly, and she complied.

It didn't take long before she arched her back and cried out as she came against me. Her walls squeezed onto me tightly, and I threw my head back as I roared out her name as my orgasm ripped through me. I knew it wouldn't take me long. I had been ready to burst since before her second orgasm.

Once I caught my breath, I left her to grab a towel and wiped up between her legs. Her stomach gurgled, and I smiled.

"I'm thinking we order some Chinese food and then spend the rest of the day not leaving this bed."

She curled up on the bed with a satisfied smile and nodded. "That sounds like the perfect day to me."

18

Sergeant Massey

The Monday morning alarm was a rude awakening to an otherwise perfect weekend. I groaned and slapped at the nightstand, only to realize it was on Riley's side of the bed. He rolled over and smacked the thing until it went silent before turning towards me and pulling me back into his arms. He moved me closer as he muttered something adorably incomprehensible and nuzzled my neck.

"Mmm, good morning." He sighed, running his lips along my neckline. I leaned back into him, rubbing my backside against his growing erection, then paused when he asked, "Are you ready to go to work?"

I groaned and pulled the blanket over my head, protecting myself, and he chuckled and tore it off me as he pinned me underneath him. He eased himself between my legs and teased my mound with the head of his cock.

"You're pretty lively this morning," I noted breathlessly, and he leaned in for a kiss.

He ground his hardness against me and brushed his fingers over my nipples. I gasped and arched into him. "Careful, my boss might not like it if I'm late."

He let out a low chuckle against my throat and stroked his thumbs over my nipples as he teased me. "He might be okay if it's only a few minutes."

My protests were lost as he pushed his cock between my wet lips and pressed against my clit. I reached my hands up above my head and dug my fingers into the sheets in preparation. He slipped his cock inside me and I moaned, biting down on his shoulder as he filled me up.

Riley took his time moving in and out of me and I moved my hips along with him, hoping that would signal for him to move faster.

"I might be able to excuse your tardiness in exchange for a small favor."

I glanced back at him, my eyebrows raised. "Oh yeah? What's that?"

He paused in his rhythm a moment as he leaned down to put his lips next to my ear.

"At work today, I want you to show up wearing your shortest skirt with no panties. I want you to come into my office and bend over, right beside me."

"Y-yes, sir." I confirmed, and he groaned, picking up the pace, pumping faster and harder into me.

I was surprised that I wasn't sore at all. In fact, the idea of behaving so salaciously in the office got me even more excited, and I rocked my hips back against him even harder.

He told me to rub my pussy, which I barely heard as I felt myself approaching climax. I reached my hand down and just brushed over my clit when I was thrown over the edge.

Riley stroked a hand over one of my breasts and pinched my nipple. The sensation was overwhelming. I had barely recovered from the first one when his pounding in and out of me and continued nipple play had me feeling a second orgasm building.

As he came deep in me, I was pushed over the edge again, and my hips bucked up as I unraveled completely. He left me breathless and shattered as he pulled himself out of me minutes later.

I lay breathless and overwhelmed as he mentioned something about taking a shower as he finished wiping me up, warning me not to follow him. I could already feel the soreness growing between my legs. I knew if I followed him into the shower that I wouldn't be able to leave. If he gave me a third orgasm this morning, I was sure my legs would give out.

He kissed me passionately before he left and told me he would have coffee ready for me downstairs and I should take my time coming into work. I let out a long sigh once he left me alone and stared at the ceiling with my arms still above me.

This was the most amazing weekend I had ever had. Even if it was over, I knew this thing I had started with the colonel was far from it. Every kiss and touch only made me want him more. My body yearned for him when he wasn't here, and I was beginning to need him as much as I wanted him. I was falling in love with him, just as I had forbidden myself from doing. I wanted sex from him, but also, I wanted more from him.

An insuppressible smile worked its way onto my lips, and I curled my knees up to my chest and hugged myself as I rolled on my side.

I allowed myself to get lost in my thoughts for only a few more minutes before I dragged myself out of bed and forced myself to get ready for work.

I was tender in many places, but I still wanted him. Though I knew I was running extra late today, I still wanted to pick up a particular item of clothing from my house in preparation for work today. It had been stored away in my uniform bag for the better part of the last four years, but it would be my secret weapon for driving Riley wild in the office.

Most of this weekend, I had allowed him to be in control and I followed his lead. However, now I wanted to take back a little bit of that control. I wanted to tease him and get him riled up like he had been doing to me.

Every brush of his fingers over my skin and featherlight kiss on my lips had me dripping. I wanted to see the desire in his eyes and his struggle to maintain his composure in the office. I wanted him holding back every moan and desperately hiding his reactions. Just like he did to me on Friday, I would drive him crazy and leave him wanting more.

19

Colonel Lang

I wasn't expecting Nicole in bright and early as usual, but as the time for my first meeting approached, I began to worry when she hadn't shown up yet.

What if I had left her too sore to get out of bed? What if she slipped in the shower and bumped her head? I paced around the office before I finally caved and just texted her.

My phone dinged a moment later and she texted back saying she grabbed another coffee along with doughnuts, but she was almost here. I texted her back with a warning about texting and driving and didn't hear anything until ten minutes later.

She strode into the office looking like a hot mess. Her hair was sticking up in messy waves and her shirt was only partly tucked in. She wore a tight skirt that clung to her curves like a second skin. If it was just a few inches higher, I might not be able to resist myself. Still, there was no way that was standard uniform.

"Took you long enough, Sergeant," I huffed, and she waved her hand dismissively as she ignored me.

Her defiant actions lit a fire in me that I noted she would pay for later. I would teach her how to properly treat me as a submissive.

She started setting up the coffee and doughnuts in preparation for our morning meeting. I walked up behind her and ran my hand over her ass and let out a low moan. She gasped and pressed back into me. She rolled her head to the side, exposing her neck which I hungrily consumed.

"I should be the only one getting you this unraveled looking," I growled in her ear and tucked in her shirt for her.

She gave me a flirtatious look with lidded eyes and heavy lashes. She handed me a coffee before looking at her reflection in my cabinet and clipping her hair up. Her exposed neck was so kissable it was near impossible to ignore. Everything about her was a temptation. I couldn't wait for this meeting to be over.

"I'm so sorry, sir. I managed to get myself out of bed and shower, but then when I stopped by my house for a minute, my bed was so tempting that I crawled back in for fifteen minutes, and I woke up an hour later."

"Oh yeah? Rough weekend?" I asked, eyebrow raised, and she smirked.

She leaned against the counter with her legs crossed, sipping her coffee as she eyed me critically. "You could say that. I was kept up all night, and my workout this weekend was very intense." She rolled the words and ran her hand down the front of her skirt erotically.

I approached her slowly with dark eyes, and she tilted her head back to meet my gaze, tempting me. If I closed the distance between us, there wouldn't be any going back. I would have to finish us both.

A ding on her computer alerted us of an upcoming event, and her eyes widened in surprise as she remembered the rest of the world still existed outside this room. She flipped open the doughnut box and handed me a bear claw.

"Five minutes until your meeting," she said cheerfully.

As she left, she dropped some paper off her desk and bent down to grab it. I was so sure her skirt was going to rip that I was near disappointed when it didn't. My dick enjoyed it all the same.

I went back to my office, sat down at my desk, and shoved the doughnut in my mouth, something of a distraction from my thoughts of her.

I double-checked my calendar to see who my morning meeting was with and let out an audible groan of disdain. Nicole looked at me with a curious expression. When she saw it was out of disgust rather than something salacious, she seemed less interested and disappeared back around the corner.

If there was anyone who represented the blatant sexism and backwards idealism of the old realm of military the most, it was Colonel Markum. We had been butting heads since he was reassigned here about seven years ago.

Rumor had it he had been involved in several scandals that were promptly swept under the rug. If I had any more evidence than whispers, I would have been after his removal years ago. A military career did not excuse inappropriate behavior, no matter how many stars you wore.

"Colonel Lang, Colonel Markum here to see you," Nicole introduced, leading the colonel into my office, and my displeasure dissolved to a more neutral expression as he glanced around.

I noticed his eyes lingering on Nicole and clenched my teeth to keep from snarling. Markum had a reputation I wanted no part of, and I certainly wanted Nicole to have no part of it either. She was mine, and I wasn't interested in sharing her in any capacity.

20

Sergeant Massey

I was surprised how quickly his mood soured once Colonel Markum showed up. Though I didn't consider Riley to be an overly friendly guy while he was in his business mode, he was never openly hostile in any capacity that I had seen before. He was the one to keep his cool in a room full of hotheads.

Today, though, he looked two pokes away from going off. He seemed in such a good mood earlier, but now he was very clearly glowering, his eyes shooting daggers at the portly man sitting across from him.

I took my pen and paper and set up next to Riley before turning towards Colonel Markum. I personally had no opinion of the colonel. If we ever interacted at all, nothing about it stood out to me. It was rare for me to be introduced to higher ranking officers, and Riley hadn't met with him before. However, if he had done something bad enough to make Riley resent him, then I was going to go above and beyond to steer clear of him.

"Could I interest you in anything to drink or eat? We have doughnuts this morning. I could brew a cup of coffee, too, but that'll take just a few minutes."

"The wife says I should avoid sweets, unfortunately," he chuckled heartily, patting his robust stomach, "but I'd love a coffee. A cream and two sugars if you could, sweetheart."

I gave him a polite smile through clenched teeth as I nodded and left to get the coffee. My eyes flickered up to Riley, who was continuing to give him the stink eye. One of the many things I hated was being called some endearing name by my superiors rather than my rank.

On my way to the coffeepot, I heard Colonel Markum make an inappropriate comment about how my ass looked in this skirt.

I put my hand over my mouth, and my cheeks flushed bright pink in embarrassment. I should not have worn this skirt to work. I debated running home, since there was no way this was workplace appropriate attire, and he could definitely report me for wearing it. It was completely against uniform regulations. The military had a "no questions asked" policy with "no distractions," and you were given a strong written warning immediately. I had gotten one at my first duty station over my hair as strands of it had fallen out of the tight bun I had pinned up.

I composed myself and refrained from making eye contact as the coffee finished brewing and I walked back into the office.

I handed Colonel Markum the coffee, and my eyes flashed to Riley. He was livid. I kept my head down as I sat back in my seat and grabbed my pencil and notepad. I hoped he wasn't too furious with me. I wore this skirt to tease him only, but I hadn't considered how others would react to it. It was the skirt I had gotten with my first uniform back when I first enlisted. I had filled out a bit more since my slightly smaller frame at eighteen, so it was now a pain to squeeze into.

Yet, I pulled it out and put it on again because I knew how much it shaped my ass and how skintight it was. I was beginning to regret the risk I took by wearing it.

I took the minutes for the meeting as attentively as I could, but my mind kept circling back to Colonel Markum's embarrassing comment, and I was trying very hard to not let the color take over my face again. It was a tense meeting, for sure, and I thought it would boil over before the end, but Colonel Markum finally stood up and excused himself.

I led him out, and he gave me one last appraising look before I closed the door. I turned around and was face to face with Riley. I hadn't heard him come up behind me.

I yelped in surprise as his fiery eyes bored into me. He reached out and locked the door. He looked feral, and I was scared, but even more so, I was very much aroused.

"Go stand in front of my desk with your back to me," he demanded, and I let out a shaky breath in anticipation.

"Y-yes, sir." I followed his command and after a few minutes, I heard him approach from behind.

"Spread your legs, Sergeant"

I bit down on my lip as I obeyed, feeling the wetness grow between my thighs as I parted them. He ran his hand slowly up the inside of my thighs, the brushes of his fingertips barely perceptible, but it was driving me wild. His fingertips felt all the way up my dripping core. He touched my bare pussy and groaned. I smiled in satisfaction.

I had been good and kept my promise and had not worn panties for him. His finger slid between my lips and lightly circled my clit. I gasped and backed into him, feeling his cock through the thin fabric of my skirt.

"This does not seem like a regulation uniform to me, Sergeant," he growled into my ear, and I shuddered.

"N-no, sir," I gasped, and he pressed tighter into me.

"Then, I think it's time to deliver your punishment."

I couldn't hold back the moan as he eased a finger into me and found that rough patch that had me quivering.

He paused and pressed his lips against my ear. "Don't make a sound. Go close the door to my office in case you disobey. Then, I want you back in this spot with your skirt hiked up and you bent over my desk."

My legs were shaking, but I nodded meekly and muttered, "Yes, sir" as I stumbled to his door. I closed and locked it before bending over his desk, and I pulled my skirt up, spreading my legs in preparation. My face was pressed against the cool wood, and I wondered what he planned to do to me. Was he going to start fucking me right away?

His hand came down hard on my ass, and I let out a yelp of surprise. It didn't really hurt, but it was a bit of a shocking feeling when not expected. I quickly muffled my noises by biting down on my forearm.

He rubbed my ass soothingly before leaning down and whispering into my ear. "That was for teasing me."

He leaned back, and a moment later, there was another smack against my ass. This time, I was prepared, and I let out a muffled whimper. My inner thighs were probably soaked.

"That was for having such a tight skirt on. This uniform is far tighter and shorter than allowed per the army's guidelines."

The list of my transgressions was long, I knew, and I wondered if I could come solely from this. He spanked me again, a little harder, before rubbing my ass which was starting to sting a little.

"That was for being late."

My legs were trembling, barely holding my ass up towards him. Another spanking had tears stinging my eyes as my core throbbed. He rubbed where he smacked for only a moment before his index finger dipped between my ass cheeks. He teased my rosebud, and I let out a shaky breath as I rocked back against him. He slowly pushed his finger inside me, deeper this time, and I cried out as pleasure raked through me. I needed to be fucked by him now, or I would go mad.

"That was for being so damn hot in that uniform that I need to fuck you right here on my desk."

I spread my legs farther apart and whimpered, no longer caring to muffle myself. His finger moved in and out of me tantalizingly slow, and if he kept this up, I would come from this alone.

He pulled his finger out of me, and I heard his zipper being pulled down. I bit down on my lip as I smiled. I was completely his.

21

Colonel Lang

I usually considered myself a patient, levelheaded guy, but when Markum made that comment about Nicole's ass, I almost lost it. He seemed oblivious to my glare after he had made it, and by some small miracle, I managed to keep my voice even for the rest of the meeting. I hoped Nicole hadn't heard, but the red in her cheeks and the way she cast her eyes away from us indicated she did. I was worried I would break my pen as fury swirled inside me.

I kept the meeting as short as I could, but Markum was one of those people who always found something to drone on and on about, whether it was football or his latest golf match or gossip among the officers that had no business being aired out in public.

I found him annoying and distasteful, a relic of a dying realm desperate to remain relevant. That was even before he made the comment. Now, my loathing of the man was unmatched. I had never been particularly possessive in any of my relationships before this, but with Nicole, there was just something about her, and I wanted her to myself, completely and utterly.

I realized I should probably define my terms of our engagement, but as I watched Markum walk out of the office, passing another longing glance at Nicole, I knew there was something else I had to do first. I walked up behind her as she led him out and reached around her to lock the door.

That ass in her skirt had been driving me wild, and it was time for her to pay the piper. I commanded her to go stand at the front of my desk, and she scurried away obediently. Seeing her from behind as I approached her had my dick straining to bust out of my slacks.

Oh, she would definitely need to be taught a lesson about proper work attire. I already had her punishment in mind, and when I reached my hand between her legs, feeling her dripping in anticipation, I knew she was going to enjoy it.

I made a throaty comment about her skirt as I pressed into her, allowing her to feel my hardened cock. She smelled of my soap, and my dick throbbed even more. She was mine.

I demanded she close the door to my office though it would only go so far to muffle her moans. My office was in a relatively unvisited wing of the building, so I was hoping no one popped in for a surprise visit.

She got into position on my desk, and it was even better than my fantasy. She hadn't worn panties, per my instruction, and her bare ass and wet pussy gleamed at me from between her spread legs. There was nothing I could imagine more erotic at that moment. I wanted to immediately stick my dick inside her, but I didn't think that would fully impact her as much as the punishment I had planned.

I brushed my hands over her bare backside, preparing the area before winding my hand back and smacking it against her ass. She let out a yelp of surprise and I checked her face to see a satisfied smile curled on her lips.

I grinned and rubbed the soft globe where my hand made contact. I told her the first sin and she shuddered and managed a shaky "Y-yes, sir." I grabbed the desk on either side of her as I drew in a sharp breath and gripped the wood tightly. This was going to be longer for me than for her. I got back into position and prepared for her next sin.

With every spanking and moaned "Yes s-sir," my dick twitched, and I struggled to maintain control. I knew that patience gave a sweeter reward, but my body was begging for her. I wanted her—no, I *needed* her—and though I could easily lengthen the list of her transgressions, I needed to be inside her.

I pulled my finger out from inside her and unzipped my pants. She let out a sigh and spread her legs wider. This woman would be the death of me, for sure.

She was so slick that my dick slipped into her tight channel without much resistance. I sheathed myself completely inside her, and she cried out, barely muffling her moan with her forearm. I threw my head back as I held tightly to her hips, rocking against her for a moment before slowly pulling out of her. She whimpered as my head popped out and I rubbed it against her clit.

She mewled and rocked her hips back against me to gyrate against my shaft. I slapped her ass playfully, telling her to behave, and she let out a shaky laugh as her legs trembled. Her fingers gripped the edge of my wooden desk desperately, and I could see her teeth as she bit down on her forearm, trying to maintain control.

I circled my dick around her clit and then teased at her opening again, and she moaned loudly as she stretched back onto me. I leaned over her, my dick pulling halfway out, and she whimpered again in protest.

"You better keep it down, or someone might come in here to investigate all this noise," I warned, and her eyes widened, meeting mine, and she bit down on her lip. My dick twitched.

"I can't help it, sir, you're going to make me come," she protested, and I suppressed the urge to growl.

I wanted her to come on my dick, but I also wanted to watch her try to hold it back as long as she could. "Hold it, Massey, you'll come with me and only then," I commanded, and she looked up at me with pleading eyes. I pushed my dick deep inside her, and she gasped, tensing as she clenched her muscles. "That's an order."

She moaned softly, and her muscles gripped my dick tightly, but she was holding back her orgasm. I half-wanted her to fall apart and come despite herself, but I knew the moment she did that it would push me over the edge with her, and I wasn't quite ready to let go of this feeling yet. This was the stuff that brought even the strongest man to his knees, and she had me there.

22

Sergeant Massey

Pleasure tremored its way through me, and I shuddered with every thrust of his dick. I was desperate to come, but he had commanded me to wait for him, and I was even more desperate to obey. I could feel his dick twitching inside me even as he forbade me from coming, but I knew he was close. His dick was hitting every sensitive spot inside me, and it was as if he was goading me into disobeying him.

It was through sheer power of will that I was able to hold on for a few more thrusts, but I could feel his sex throbbing inside me. He must have been torturing himself as well.

"Nicole, come on my dick, that's an order," he groaned, and all at once, I let go, and the pleasure whisked me away.

I bit my lip to muffle the cries of my orgasm and tasted copper. I could feel myself unraveling as if he was pulling the string and I had lost control completely. My mind was shattered as my muscles clamped down around him and spasmed. He thrust deeply inside me and moaned as his cock swelled and spurted. The orgasm was one of my longest, and it felt like minutes passed before I was left a quivering mess in front of him.

"Gods, Massey, you're going to kill me," he panted, pressing against me as he cocooned me with his body.

I smiled and melted against him. "You're quite insatiable yourself, sir," I teased, breathlessly, and he chuckled, trailing his lips over my shoulder blade.

He pulled out of me slowly, and I shivered. I couldn't believe my body was still craving another round. I stayed put as he wiped me up and held the towel against my sex. I jumped as he brushed it against my nether regions. I was still sensitive, but the rough texture of his gym towel was a wonderful sensation across my clit. I didn't want him to stop, but I had to remember where we were.

He pulled my skirt down over my ass and gave it a gentle pat as he sent me back towards my office. "When's my next meeting, sergeant?"

I glanced at the books and then at the clock. "That would be lunch, sir."

"Would you like to go somewhere?" he asked.

I leaned against his doorway as I thought about what I actually wanted. "I'm craving a burger but also a milkshake. I should probably go clean myself up completely first, but then, we can go someplace."

His eyes darkened, and he motioned to the desk in front of him. "Well, don't dally then, Sergeant, bring me my lunch."

My eyes widened, and my legs trembled. I didn't think I could come again after the orgasm I just had. However, as if my body was speaking for itself, I walked over and pulled my skirt back up as I lay back on his desk in front of his chair.

I shuddered at my immediate obedience as I spread my legs and stretched my arms above me. I stared up at the ceiling as his chair rolled closer to me. He lifted my legs over his shoulders and then grabbed my hips.

I closed my eyes and gasped as his lips brushed over the sensitive flesh of my inner thigh. My legs were shaking helplessly as his tongue traced over my nether lips, but he held me tightly. He stroked my sensitive bud softly, circling it and flicking against it, sending electrical bursts soaring through me. I let out soft moans as I rocked my hips in his arms.

"Oh, Riley, please…" I trailed off as I felt the tightened knot growing within me again, and he growled against my sex.

It vibrated through me, and I squirmed as I approached that blissful peak again. He had me completely at his mercy already. He must have known because he slowed his pace even as I ground my hips against his face. I whimpered in protest, and he reached his hand down to tease my sensitive rosebud.

I moaned and circled my hips, enjoying both previously neglected parts being played with. He increased the pressure of his tongue the same time as he pushed his finger inside me.

The combined sensations pushed me over the edge. I drew in a sharp breath as I arched my hips. The orgasm tore through me as I cried out without restraint, daring the outside world to take notice. He brought me down slower than he brought me up, easing me out of the orgasm and keeping his promise to clean me up as he lapped my pussy clean.

Once I was able to speak and regained control of my limbs, I thanked him and went to stand, but my legs gave way, and I stumbled into his lap. His arms held me steady against him, and I met his eyes. I could feel his dick through his uniform, and he was ready for another round after servicing me.

"Do you need some attention?" I purred and cupped his cock through his pants. It twitched against my hand, but he chuckled and shook his head, moving my hand away from him.

"You can have more of that later after work, but we need to eat actual food, and you need a break. I don't want you passing out on me. That's an order."

I grinned and kissed him. He allowed the kiss, but when I started to get greedy, he carried me and deposited me in my own chair.

"You're the insatiable one," he murmured, and with hungry eyes, I watched him stalk back into his office.

He had awoken something deviant and insatiable inside me. Before, I was empty, but he filled that hole inside me, in more ways than one. I wasn't going to stop craving him anytime soon.

23

Sergeant Massey

We managed to make it through the rest of the day without incident, but I could tell by the way that he watched me that the skirt was a big hit. My legs trembled with every step after he made me come the last time, so he assigned me to desk duty while he picked up our lunch.

He delivered on both the burger and the milkshake. I moaned appreciatively as I took a bite of the burger, and his gaze was a look of warning. I smiled to myself. I have never driven anyone as crazy as I seemed to drive him, and confidence bloomed in me. I wanted to surprise him later…and I had just the coat to do it.

I stopped by my home to ready myself before popping back over to his place. I packed another overnight bag in anticipation. An hour later, I showed up at his place with my wavy hair wild around my head and wearing nothing but flats and a peacoat. He was expecting me when he opened the door, but he eyed the coat in interest.

I stepped through the threshold and kicked the door closed behind me as I opened the coat seductively and let it fall to the floor. His eyes appraised me hungrily before he pinned me back against the door and his lips claimed mine in a searing kiss.

I pressed into him, and his hands slid over my naked skin. We were panting by the time he hitched me up by my thighs and carried me to his bedroom.

He laid me down on his bed, and I spread my legs in anticipation. He knelt between them and had me quivering with just his fingers before flipping me onto my stomach and sheathing himself inside me. It didn't take long before we were pushed over the edge and he came inside me. He fell on the bed beside me, breathless, and I locked eyes with him as we both panted.

"I can't seem to get enough of you, Nicole."

I locked my fingers with his. "Me either, Riley."

He kissed my lips softly until my stomach growled and ruined the moment. He admitted to already having made food, expecting us to eat before making our way upstairs.

I dressed in one of his T-shirts while he pulled on a pair of boxers, and we made our way downstairs. Though the food had cooled down a bit, it was still delicious. He had made an alfredo chicken dish with sautéed asparagus.

His cooking ability still amazed me. I made a mean grilled cheese sandwich, but most of my other meals came from a box—including my "famous" cheesecake, which I claimed was a family secret. I would take that fact to my grave though.

Once we finished eating, I offered to clean up, so he jumped in the shower first. There was something suddenly familiar about his place even though I had been here many times before on various errands. I felt comfortable there. I felt at home.

Suddenly, the smell of his soap became my favorite smell, and his T-shirts were collectively added to my wardrobe, whether willingly or not.

He called down when the shower was free, and I didn't realize how much I needed one until the warm water streamed its way down my sore body. I had not worked many of these muscles in two years, and now, they were protesting the sudden change in my activity level, but they had no objections earlier when Riley was pumping in and out of me.

I took a liberal time in the shower, but once I began to wrinkle, I considered my muscles soothed and shut off the water. I tied up my wet hair and wrapped a towel around me before opening the door and leaning against the door frame to admire my lover.

Riley lay on top of the sheets, spread out in his naked glory. He glanced up at me and smiled, patting the empty space beside him. "Drop the towel and come lie down."

I left the towel in a pile on the floor as I went to him. I felt his eyes caressing every inch of my naked form as I made my way over to him and crawled up next to him in bed. I felt like prey willingly falling right into the trap of a dangerous predator. I prepared my body for another round but was pleasantly surprised and appreciative of the sincere adoration in his eyes as they met mine.

He pulled me into him as he rolled onto his side and enveloped me with his body. I sighed and hummed pleasantly as I molded against him. He held me close while his eyes traced the features of my face with apt interest, and a blush bloomed in my cheeks. His fingers followed his eyes, tracing over the bridge of my nose, the sharp bones of my cheeks, the soft skin of my brow, and, finally, the sensitive, swollen flesh of my bottom lip.

My heart swelled at his tenderness then sped up as he groaned and leaned in to kiss me passionately. My body reacted with every touch of his lips and tongue against mine as he moved it along with mine with a slow intensity that reminded me of the first time we danced together. It was more tender than our first kiss, filled with unspoken promises and love as opposed to unabated desire.

He wrapped an arm around me as he deepened the kiss, but dizziness fluttered over me with the butterflies in my stomach, and I begrudgingly pushed him away to catch my breath.

His eyes glanced between mine with concern. "Everything all right?" he asked, and the intensity of his gaze caused me to cast my eyes away, but he hooked a finger under my chin and pulled my eyes back to his.

"Yes, I…" I trailed off, a goofy smile on my lips as I traced the features of the face I most adored. "You took my breath away."

His eyes lit up with equal affection, and he stroked his thumb over my cheek. "I can say the same about you."

He ran a hand down my arm and intertwined his fingers with mine, and he then rolled back onto his back and looked up at the ceiling. I stared up at it with him, my eyes mesmerized with patterns as his thumb caressed the back of my hand gently and soothingly. Unsaid words hung in the air, and I worried he would leave them unspoken, but then, he continued.

"I thought that my ex-wife was the only one who could make me feel such equal aching in my heart as my dick. None of my previous relationships or flings really sparked any sort of excitement within me except for a quick, passionate night, but as the moon disappeared to welcome in the day, so left the feelings and the women. With you, though, it's different.

"Excuse me if this is cheesy, but it feels worse to keep the words trapped inside only my mind. You do something to me—unlike anything I've experienced before. Not with my wife nor anyone before or after that. The morning is welcomed now, and I find you as irresistible as the night before. There's nothing more that I want than to have you here with me, sharing my bed long into the morning hours. So please, Nicole, stay the night with me…again."

Emotion poured through me, and I could barely contain the joy at hearing those words. His proposal was so pure that I didn't have the heart to tell him I had already packed my overnight bag and this was my intention all along. So, I simply told him I would be here until he told me to leave. He chuckled and told me he better clear out a drawer for me then.

He pulled the covers over us as he pulled me into his arms. I snuggled against his side, hiding my insuppressible smile against his chest.

Despite my earlier reservations, I had thrown caution to the wind, and I was falling, helplessly and desperately. Falling harder than I ever had before. Perhaps, this would be the greatest love story of us. Or, perhaps, this would hold my worst heartbreak. But I found the reward far exceeded the risk, so I would be head over heels as we stumbled further into whatever this thing we had was.

24

Colonel Lang

The rest of the week flew by blissfully. My days were filled with meetings, but my nights were filled with Nicole. She came in like a hurricane, and my life would never be the same.

Before I met her, the weekends were just another part of the cycle of the week where I could catch up on my home tasks and maybe a good book before heading back into work bright and early Monday morning, but now, I desperately embraced the fleeting minutes of those two days that were exclusively with her. Alarm clocks did not threaten our serenity, and responsibilities passed us by as we continued to get lost in each other.

This particular Saturday was one of those lazy days that I wanted to persist infinitely. The sun had long ascended by the time we dragged ourselves begrudgingly from the warmth of the other's embrace to go downstairs for brunch. Though I would have loved to spend the whole day in bed, I had prepared a surprise for her and it unfortunately involved clothes and leaving the house. If she had any objections, her curiosity outweighed them, and she followed me out to the car, and I drove us to the small, local airport where I owned a hangar.

"Wait, you own a *what?*" she stammered as we pulled up outside, and I grinned.

"I have a couple classic cars and planes that I store here. I enjoy flying or taking a drive in my downtime. I've never brought a woman here, but, well, like I said, you're different."

Her eyes were glowing with anxious anticipation as I stepped out of the car onto the airstrip and looped around to open her door.

"Well, okay, then, Mr. President. Lead the way."

I snorted and led her into the hangar. The attendant was finishing the inspections of my planes, so I led Nicole around to look at the cars. She knew a surprising amount of the older models, and she admitted to having tried and failed to fix up a couple of her dad's old cars before she left for the army. Whenever she discussed her father, her eyes distanced themselves with a nostalgic glaze, and I wondered what memory had swept her away. Her lips quirked up into a slight smile as her fingers slid over the hood. She glanced up at me and focused back in, smiling brightly.

"So, which one of these bad boys are we taking for a spin?" she asked, eyeing a '69 Boss 302 Mustang, and I pointed towards the planes.

"Well, I was thinking we'd take one of those." Her eyes followed my fingers and widened.

"Seriously?" she exclaimed, and the attendant gave me the thumbs-up, indicating I was good to go.

I motioned for her to follow me, and she dashed ahead of me to admire them. She was particularly interested in a refurbished Cessna, so I had it towed out. I helped her climb in the cockpit and buckled her in before getting myself settled.

"I can't believe you know how to fly one of these, let alone own one. You continue to amaze me, Colonel."

I grinned as she leaned forward, excitement pouring out of her as her eyes took in everything. She studied me as I did the pre-check and prepared for takeoff. I got the go-ahead to get in the air, and she gripped her seat tightly as I got us accelerating, and soon, we were off. She squealed in delight as we peeled away from the ground. The roar of the engine and propeller was familiar as it reacted to my controls, and with Nicole sitting next to me, staring at the rolling landscape in awe, it felt like this was where I was meant to be.

Below us, people carried on in their dot-sized cars, completely unaware of what happened above them, and for the first time, it felt like we were completely and utterly alone. Up here, we were untouchable. It didn't matter what I said or did or if I allowed my eyes to linger on her far too long to be appropriate. Nobody would find us or see us or hear us.

When we were at a steady glide, I locked the controls and reached out and grabbed her hand. It was difficult to truly convey the full depth of emotion that I felt right now, but as her fingers meshed with mine and squeezed, I knew she felt the same way. We locked eyes and the rest of the world melted away. I wished we could stay up here forever. I wished we could keep flying into the horizon and not look back, but reality would catch up with us eventually, so we would have to fall back to earth. I released her hand as I took the controls back and grinned. For now, though, we would fly.

*****

Her laughter was bright and comforting as the morning sun. After we had as much alone time as we could before my fuel gauge indicated it was time to head home, we landed back at the airport, and I took her to another one of my frequent spots: a nearby diner nestled comfortably in the middle of nowhere.

It lacked the elegance and convenience of most spots the officers preferred, so I knew we wouldn't have been interrupted here. My usual waitress was off, so I was spared the curious glances laced with a tinge of judgment or jealousy. I felt relaxed, and I could tell Nicole was less tense as well. I decided to entertain her with one of my favorite memories during my time in the army.

"It's a true story, swear to God. Seymour had just enough experience to get us up in the air and keep us there, so Andrew and I concocted the elaborate heist of stealing their pride and joy, *Baby Bird.*

"We proved them wrong that army men didn't know how to fly a plane. However, they never specified that army men needed to know how to *land* the plane. When it came time to touch down, we realized we had gotten ourselves in way over our heads."

Nicole's eyes widened, and she leaned forward in excitement. "So, then what happened?"

"Well, Seymour probably would have let his pride be the death of him, but Andrew and I weren't so inclined, so we admitted our dilemma. I've never heard a room full of airmen go so quiet. They asked us if we were joking, but when they realized we weren't, they scrambled to find an experienced pilot nearby to talk us out of the air. It was the most humbling thirty seconds of dead air I've ever experienced.

138

"We thought they would leave us out to dry, but eventually, they found a colonel who, between several lectures and more cusswords than I thought one man capable of knowing, managed to get us on the ground. Though, there were several close calls.

"He continued to chew us and the airmen out for an hour after we landed, but we were just grateful to be alive."

When our superior found out what we had done, he assigned us bathroom duty for the next three months. Once we finished our punishment without complaint, he paid for us all to go get our pilot's licenses. I was the only one who took him up on the offer. I don't think Seymour or Andrew ever wanted to be in the pilot's seat ever again."

Nicole erupted into laughter throughout my story that nearly brought her to tears. When she calmed down, she wiped her eyes and grinned at me. My heart beamed with joy at such a sight. She was so beautiful.

"I can't even imagine what other shenanigans you and your buddies got into if that's what you consider a 'mild' story." She leaned forward, pulling her straw between her lips, as she sucked the last bit of milkshake from her glass.

"Well, most of it is classified, but maybe I'll write a book about it someday. Something like *Catch-22* with a mix of stories—some true and others fictional—that'll leave you guessing which ridiculous tales actually happened."

She gave me a challenging look, daring me to write it, but after she noisily slurped at the last few drops through the straw, she ran her tongue over her bottom lip, and her look changed to something else entirely.

I waved down the waitress to cash ourselves out before hurrying us back home.

I stopped by Nicole's place and reminded her to grab a suitcase for our conference trip in a few days, which would involve us flying cross-country with other officers and their attendants. It would mean basically no alone time for a few days. Therefore, I would have to enjoy what alone time we would have before then.

"Unless, of course, I use my extensive, army-grade stealth training to sneak pass the guards and into your room." She countered my thought, and I smirked, shaking my head.

"I wish. Unfortunately, we must be on our best behavior. With creeping eyes on officers like Colonel Markum, any interactions deemed unprofessional will somehow find its way through the chain of command in the form of gossip. I'd really like to keep our relationship out of the limelight," I admitted, and I could see something sink inside her as disappointment flashed in her downcast eyes.

I reached out and grabbed her hand, giving her a reassuring smile. "Not that I'm embarrassed of you. I just mean that it would be best to keep us a secret for the time being. An internal affairs investigation is the last thing we need. I'm sure you don't want a ding on your record, no matter how long you have left of your enlistment."

She huffed in defeat and squeezed my hand. She stroked her thumb over the sensitive flesh on the back on my hand, watching her own movements curiously. "No, of course, I agree. It just stinks that I won't have you again until Friday. I might go through withdrawals."

Her eyes flashed up to mine, and she bit her lip. I resisted the urge to groan as I put the car in gear and floored it back home.

The checklist of items I planned to pack in her check bag would ensure that didn't happen. Even if I wouldn't physically be there to stimulate Nicole's body, I would certainly be making sure it was well stimulated.

25

Colonel Lang

The rest of the weekend flew by in a flash, and the next thing I knew, we were begrudgingly boarding our flight. It wasn't a long flight, but I felt the need to take her back to the airplane bathroom and introduce her to the mile-high club, like I longed to do during our private flight.

Unfortunately, I recognized one of the officers on our flight, so I maintained the façade of complete professionalism, but the text messages I privately shared with Nicole were anything but.

We checked in to the hotel and were pleased to find our rooms right next to each other. It would certainly be a temptation having her so close.

I sent her ahead to get situated in her room as a few officers waved to me from the bar. I noticed Markum among them, talking the ear off a young waitress who looked like she'd rather be anywhere else.

I caught Markum's attention, and he dismissed her. She shot me a grateful look before darting away. Markum was a weasel in more than just looks. He enjoyed preying on women, especially those of lower ranks. He was more than happy to wave his power around to con them into submitting to him. I would be keeping a close eye on Nicole around him, for sure. If I was lucky, I'd have the opportunity to catch him and get him booted out of the army.

I kept my greetings quick and promised to join them after I dropped off my bags. Markum's eyes followed me as I left, and I had the feeling he'd be counting the minutes until my return.

I quickly got settled into my room before knocking on Nicole's door. She opened it, and her smile immediately brightened my souring mood.

"Hey, listen, I'm going to get a drink at the bar with some of the others and catch up on the details of the conference."

"Oh, I'd love a drink!" She perked up, grabbing a sweater, and I stopped her exit.

There was no way I could let her be near an inebriated Markum. Even if it was for her own benefit, I knew I'd probably be unable to control myself if he made another comment in front of her.

"Why don't you just order some room service? You can add it to my tab. Just relax in here for a bit and I'll check on you later. Maybe we can grab dinner around then."

"Are you sure? I don't mind joining you at the bar."

"No, please. You should get some rest before tomorrow. We have meetings all day, and I need you sharp."

She nodded slowly, her eyes pained and disappointed again. "Yeah, okay, rest sounds good."

She closed the door before I could think of a way to explain that I was just trying to protect her, and I winced. I would have to explain myself later.

Back at the bar, I sat with the group and ordered myself a whiskey. Usually a drink would help me unwind after a long day, but I was very tense with my colleagues, considering I had the unfortunate luck of getting stuck right next to Markum. I wasn't feeling very social, which he took advantage of, as he leaned towards me.

"That Massey is a hell of a looker. You really hit the jackpot there. I'm jealous of your arm piece, Lang. I wish I had one as fine as yours."

I glared at him as I took a sip of my whiskey. "I'm not sure what you're implying, but my secretary is off-limits to both of us. What you're suggesting is out of line and against the UCMJ, so I suggest you keep those thoughts to yourself." I paused before I narrowed my eyes. "Or better yet, let's not have them at all."

Markum rolled his eyes, his lips twisted in a malicious smirk. "Sure thing, Lang. Keep your secrets, but I can tell you if I had a secretary like her, I'd have claimed her long ago. Unless you're fine with sharing her, of course."

He winked at me as I grabbed my glass tightly, jerking up with wild eyes. Markum left me then to chase down the waitress once more, and I found a way to insert myself into the conversation.

I kept my voice and expression even, but inside, I was raging. Markum tested my patience like nothing else, and I didn't like what he was suggesting at the end there. If he tried to lay a finger on Nicole, I'd take his whole arm. She was mine, and even if she wasn't, she was far too good for a sleazeball like Markum.

Once the conversation shifted away from my areas of expertise into the realm of rumors, Markum returned, and I pulled out my phone, texting Nicole and instructing her to check her bag for the little presents I left for her.

Not long after I texted Nicole, she responded.

Nicole: Wow, Colonel! I'll have you know this is a work trip and I promised to maintain the utmost aura of professionalism.

I smirked, glancing up at the group to see if any were paying attention to me, but they were all too engaged in stories about the idiotic antics of the new recruits.

Me: Oh? Is that so, sergeant? Well, that's a shame. I was hoping we could have some fun.

I pictured her biting her lip as she ruffled through the assortment of toys I had packed for her, clenching her thighs as she grew slick at the thought of stuffing them inside her.

Nicole: Which one should I use first?

Before I could write back, she messaged again.

Nicole: Sir.

I longed to join her, but my absence would be more noted than just my lack of attentiveness.

Me: How fast do you want to cum?

Nicole: Let's set a new record.

I could almost hear the challenge in her voice.

Me: Grab the purple one, and spread your legs nice and wide.

Nicole: Like this?

A picture followed soon after from the perspective of her head looking down between her spread legs. A thin, lacy red thong was the only clothing featured in the picture. I drew in a sharp breath and shifted my position as my erection rose to full mast.

I looked up to see if anyone was paying attention to me and smiled when I could see that I was still being ignored.

Me: You gotta remove the panties, or it won't work as well.

I imagined her rolling her eyes. A moment later, another picture came. This time, the panties were thrown on the edge of the bed, and I could see the well-kept patch of hair between her legs.

I longed to be between them. I *wanted* to be between them badly, pressing the vibrator against her clit as she squirmed and moaned for me. For now, I could only imagine what she was doing right now, and it made my dick throb harder.

Me: Great, now flick your nipples so you're nice and wet.

Nicole: I'm so soaked, sir. What do I do now?

I downed the rest of my drink and excused myself to go to the bathroom. I closed myself off in a stall and pushed my pants and boxers down and then grabbed my dick, barely suppressing a groan. With the other hand, I typed back a one-handed reply.

Me: Now click the button on the toy and press it against your clit. Lightly at first, just circle your clit and tease yourself just like I would.

In my head, she gasped as she pressed the vibrator against her clit and squirmed as she circled it. She would feel the heat rise in her and the knot tightening in her core.

Nicole: I think it's working. I wish it was you here. I miss your dick already. I feel so empty.

I slowly stroked myself and shuddered.

Me: Go through your toys. Stick the bigger shaft inside you, and leave the smaller one pressed against your clit. Imagine it's my dick inside you and your finger on your clit.

The thought of her fucking herself while thinking about me thrusting my dick inside her was almost enough to make me come instantly. I was sensitive at this moment, and I knew that if I was with her, I'd be on edge.

Nicole: Mmm, Riley, I feel it. Can you step away for a minute?

I debated telling her that I was already hiding from the others, but instead, I just double-checked the other stalls were empty before locking myself away again and calling her.

"I'm so close." Her voice quivered as she answered, and I knew she was.

I picked up the pace of my hand and tightened my grip around my shaft. "Come with me," I commanded, and she squeaked, and I heard the creaking of the bed.

I closed my eyes and pictured her arching her back as she quickly slid the vibrator in and out of her dripping pussy, rolling her hips so it hit all the right spots.

She let out a soft whimper, and the phone thudded as if she knocked it off the bed. It pushed me over the edge, and I came, shooting my load into the toilet. She grabbed the phone after a minute, still panting as she put it up to her ear. "Thank you, sir," she breathed, her voice still shaky, before she hung up, and I smiled proudly to myself.

I had a woman who I could make come with just a phone call. It would be hard to resist sneaking over to her room tonight, but the phone call gave me a good idea for what we could do instead.

I quickly cleaned myself up before joining the other officers again. They seemed to take little notice of my absence except for Markum, who gave me a curious glance.

Whatever drama he was hoping to start, I would do everything in my power to keep it from reaching Nicole. She'd had enough shit cards dealt to her throughout her time with the army. I wasn't going to let her last year of enlistment be mucked up by the result of my carelessness.

26

Sergeant Massey

The hotel room was massive, and I scoffed for a moment at the luxury afforded to the officers and their support staff when traveling. I soon dismissed the thought as I jumped into the massive bed and got lost in the comforter. I was at risk of falling asleep when a knock sounded at the door. I suppressed a groan and opened the door to Riley standing on the other side with a hard-to-read look. My expression changed to a bright smile.

He told me he was going to have a drink with the other officers. I thought about how refreshing having a nice, cold beer would be with the other officers and their secretaries, so I reached for my jacket.

He then suggested I just order room service, and I thought he noticed my tired look from being moments from a nap, but I really wanted a drink right now. When he was persistent about me not coming though, I got the message.

Ah, so it's a boys' club only event. Disappointment settled in. A tinge of jealousy sparked within me, but I quickly smothered it. I had played these games before and only gotten burned. I was just a secretary, and I would do my duty until I could get out of the army. I couldn't let my fear of missing out get the best of me now. Getting involved had only ever gotten me into trouble. I had to be on my best behavior and avoid drawing attention to myself...or to the colonel, for that matter. The army liked soldiers who didn't create ripples. The unwritten motto was keep your head down and your shoulders straight.

I was still a little sore from his rejection, so I ordered a special treat for myself off the room service menu and charged it all to his room. I hopped into bed and watched TV while I ate. The food was delicious. This was the high life for sure. Mr. "I own a hanger for *planes*" probably was used to this treatment. I wondered if this was what I could expect from a life with him. Blissful luxury in the form of chocolate-covered strawberries that made your whole body zing.

I quickly squashed the thoughts of a long-term future with the colonel. Those were dangerous thoughts. Both for my feelings and for our jobs. If I got too caught up in us, I'd end up slipping up sometime and get us caught.

My enlistment was almost over, and Riley had been in for his whole life. It would be bad for his career and would certainly mar my record. A dishonorable discharge when the finish line was so close would put a hefty damper on my future plans. I would do my best to behave.

I bit my lip as I smiled to myself, wondering if the colonel would be able to behave himself. Curse those delicious strawberries that left a persistent arousal.

As if on cue, my phone dinged with a message from Riley.

Riley: Have you gone through your bags, yet? I packed you a surprise.

My fears were confirmed when I searched my check bag to find a pouch full of various toys. Embarrassment left me hot in the face as I imagined the look on the airport security's face as they inspected my bags with my uniforms and then a bag of pleasure toys.

I hid my head under the blanket while I recovered, but then, curiosity overcame the shame, and I rummaged through the bag. There were a lot of interesting items in there and some of which I had absolutely no idea what to do with.

I grabbed my phone and instinctively typed a sassy response. I regretted it as soon as I sent it because I wasn't really looking to behave at this particular moment, so I quickly followed up his response with something more encouraging.

His next question had my eyes widening and wetness pooling between my legs in anticipation. He directed me towards a purple one that I grabbed before stuffing the rest back into the bag and setting it on the floor.

I flicked it on and off, and it vibrated enticingly in my hand. I quivered at the thought of pressing it against my clit. I propped up the pillows and lay on my back with my legs spread. I bit my lip as I decided he needed a tease as much as I did.

I quickly snapped a picture and then waited for the colonel's next command. I snorted at his response and stripped down before snapping a spicier picture, careful to keep any identifying information out of the shot.

His next instruction came in quickly, and I brushed my thumb and forefinger over my nipples, but I didn't really need any help getting wet—I was already soaked. I sent him back a hurried reply when my legs started trembling.

I followed his instructions to a T, adding in my own flourishes that caused my eyes to roll back in my head. The vibrator filled me up as I slid it inside me, and I bucked on the bed. It wasn't as good as his cock, but my muscles clenched around it tightly, and I knew I was close. Texting wouldn't cut it anymore if he expected me to last long.

A few moments later, I was desperately trying to contain myself as the vibrator on my clit and the one in my pussy were overwhelming.

He finally called, and I could only manage a few words before my words garbled into intangible moans. He said the golden words, and I cried out as euphoria sluiced through me, leaving behind crashing tremors of pleasure.

I heard him grunting through the haze, and the echo of his voice made me realize he had stepped into the bathroom. It made me feel so much naughtier that he had been texting me with his coworkers mere feet away.

We both came down, and there was no more sound other than our breaths heavy through the receiver and the steady vibrations of the toys. I finally shut them off as my body relaxed, and I thanked him in a low, throaty purr before hanging up.

I pulled the vibrator out of me with a wet pop and stretched out with a satisfied smile on the sheets. I curled up into a ball against the pillows and figured it wouldn't hurt to get a few moments' rest after that intense orgasm. I sighed pleasantly and let sleep blanket me.

*****

My slumber was interrupted by my cell phone ringing. I first thought it might be an alarm, but when I heard Riley's voice after I swiped to answer, I put the receiver against my ear with a lazy smile. "Mmm, hello," I greeted him drowsily, my voice cracking as I rubbed the sleep out of my eyes.

"Did I wake you?" he asked, his voice light with amusement.

I yawned as I stretched out before curling back into a ball around the phone. "You did, but that's okay. I might have dozed off after you called. What time is it?"

"It's 1800 hours. Are you hungry? I know this little restaurant down the street, and I'd like to take you to dinner."

My eyes widened, and I jerked up into a sitting position. "Really? I thought we were behaving?"

I could almost hear him smirking through the phone by the tone of his voice. "We are, of sorts. You still have to eat, Sergeant Be ready in half an hour. That's an order."

"Yes, sir!" I said before hanging up.

I needed to clean myself up before we left, so I rolled out of bed and dashed to the shower. I was grateful that I had allotted myself one fun outfit for this trip as I had the one option that was perfect for the climate but would drive the colonel wild. He deserved it for getting me all worked up on a work trip.

27

Colonel Lang

Nicole was absolutely stunning in the knee-length floral print dress with free-flowing fabric that swayed with every movement. It was short enough that I knew with her sitting that it would ride just high enough that ... I shook my head at my thoughts, but as she looked up at me with dark, teasing eyes and her lips pursed in a deliciously tempting fashion, I knew she had worn it precisely for this reason.

I approached her and glanced in either direction down the hallway, finding that we were alone. I pinned her against the wall between my arms and leaned in to press my lips against her ear.

"Take off your panties, Nicole," I demanded and leaned back to see the widening of her eyes before her lips turned up in a mischievous smirk.

She glanced around before lifting her skirt, her eyes not leaving my face as she did so. My cock was throbbing as I watched her hook her thumbs into the waistband of her panties. She bit her lip as she slowly slid them down her long legs and then stepped out of them and handed them to me. It was a lacy, red thong, and I suppressed a groan as I tightened my fist around them and felt the dampness in the silky fabric. She turned to walk down the hallway, but I pulled her back into me so she could feel the hardness of my cock against her backside for just a moment.

"You drive me crazy." My breath was heavy against her ear as I nipped at her earlobe.

She gasped as my lips trailed over her shoulder before I pulled away abruptly and started walking towards the exit. She huffed in her frazzled state, and I smirked. *Two could play at this game, Nicole.*

Fortunately, the restaurant was close enough that I didn't have to get us a car, and we walked down the street a short distance.

It was not too chilly, but it was getting to that time of year when dusk swallowed the sun far earlier. Nicole paused a moment to catch a glimpse of the bright colors dancing through the sky while I simply took the moment to watch her.

She glanced over at me and blushed, casting her gaze back towards the ground. I risked a moment of affection as I hooked my arm in hers and walked her down the street to the restaurant before releasing her. I got us a table that was more private, nestled in the back where the lighting was dimmed and the seating was more intimate.

The waiter brought us menus, and I ordered a wine I thought might catch Nicole's fancy. When the waiter left, Nicole gave me a longing stare before opening her menu. I gave her a few moments of silence until the waiter brought us the wine. She took a hesitant sip, but when I got her nod of approval, I instructed him to leave the bottle.

We ordered our food and made idle chitchat while drinking. Nicole was taking generous sips of her wine, and it wasn't long until I poured her a second glass. Her cheeks quickly became flushed and her eyes heavier as the alcohol settled in her. My hand brushed her thigh as I laid my napkin in my lap, and she gasped.

I smirked and leaned into her. "Why, Massey, are you turned on right now?"

She looked down at her plate, and the flush spread down her neck and along her collarbone. "Yes," she whispered breathlessly and bit down on her bottom lip as her eyes met mine. If looks could kill.

Before I could reach my hands over to touch her, the waiter brought us our food. I started into my steak, and she nibbled on hers, but I could tell her mind was elsewhere. I glanced around and it didn't look like anyone was paying any attention our way. I dipped my hand below the table and found the bare skin of her knee. She gasped as my fingers traced gingerly up the inside of her soft legs and her breath shook as my hand disappeared underneath her skirt.

She spread her legs on reflex, and I found my way to her dripping mound. She sucked in a sharp breath and quickly bit down on her lip again to quiet herself. I wanted to bite that lip. The desire made me bolder as I dipped a finger between her nether lips and circled her clit with a tantalizingly slow finger. After her breaths grew ragged, I slid the finger back inside her, and she trembled.

She was soaked long before I even started touching her, and my dick to throbbed in want. I needed this woman. She was so close I was worried she would come right away as my finger slowly slid in and out of her, but I was also afraid she wouldn't be able to stay quiet. She needed something else to focus on.

"Try to finish your dinner," I commanded softly, calmly, though my insides were hot with desire for her.

"I don't know if I can." Her voice was breathless as she met my eyes.

Her fingers were gripping the seat of the chair so tightly her knuckles were white. I pulled my finger out of her and drew lazy circles on the inside of her thigh to calm her down. "Yes, it is quite hard," I teased, and she rolled her eyes, but her lips twitched up in the corners.

She picked up a bite of her food and chewed on it a moment. "You're not making this easy."

"No, I'm not, but neither were you when you handed me a wet thong."

Her eyes twinkled with mischief. I brushed my finger over her clit again, and she gasped, dropping the fork. Oh God, she was sensitive. She was so close to coming. I let out a possessive growl as I pressed into her bud, and her legs shook, and her fingers twisted into the fabric of her skirt.

"Well, look who it is. Riley and his lovely secretary."

I quickly moved my hand out from between her legs, and she fixed her skirt when we heard Markum from a distance. I turned and saw him making his way towards our table. Rage bubbled inside of me, and I didn't bother suppressing my glare. This asshole's timing was impeccable.

28

Sergeant Massey

I was almost there. I was so fucking close. My insides were all clenched up and my head was spinning as the orgasm threatened to pull me under. The colonel almost had me coming here in front of the whole restaurant. Then that creep had to ruin it.

Riley became tense as Markum approached our table. He growled under his breath, and I knew he was just as annoyed as I was. If Markum had just waited ten more seconds…

Then he would have seen me come. The thought made my cheeks redden in embarrassment. That was risky and unbelievably close. I needed a moment to get myself put back together so as soon as Markum pulled up a chair to the table, I excused myself to the restroom. I didn't want Markum to see me any more undone than he already did, but hopefully, most of it was hidden in the dim lighting.

I splashed cold water on my face the moment I was in the bathroom and stared at myself in the mirror as it dripped down my face and neck. That was way too close. Yet I still had the urge to continue where the colonel had left off. I was so close, and my body was almost there... As if on cue, my phone buzzed.

Riley: Don't you dare come, Sergeant!

I let out an aggravated groan. "Damn it!" My hand tightened around my phone as the urge to throw it across the room was strong. I splashed more water on me to cool myself down and leaned back against the sink. It was unfair of him to request that of me after he had gotten me so heated up. I relieved my bladder to buy myself some more time before I straightened out my dress and fixed my hair. I wished I had my underwear now.

Markum was still sitting at our table when I returned. I gave him a polite smile as I sat down, but my eyes shot him daggers at the way his eyes were fixated on my breasts. Though I hadn't eaten much of my meal, I lost my appetite. Markum's eyes never left me, and I wished I had the courage to call him out on it, but I just glanced at Riley uncomfortably.

"Colonel Lang, thank you for the dinner, but I'm afraid I'm not feeling well. Do you mind if I return back to my room?"

His eyes softened sympathetically, and he nodded, lifting his hand to get the waiter's attention. I rose while Riley sorted out the bill, and Markum rose as well.

"I hope you feel better soon, Sergeant I apologize for interrupting your evening."

His eyes had no room for sorrow with the knowing gleam, and I had never so strongly felt the urge to punch a superior. That would be a quick way to end my military career, for sure.

Instead, I gave him another half-hearted smile which quickly disappeared as I turned on my heels and left the restaurant. Riley followed closely, but I didn't slow until I was able to shake the feeling of Markum's eyes on my backside. The night temperature had dropped considerably, or maybe the restaurant was just hot, as the air cooled the fire burning inside me as well.

I let out a long sigh, and Riley stepped up behind me.

"I'm sorry about that, Nicole."

His sincerity caused me to turn. My eyes softened, and the anger drained out of my face. "It's all right. We knew better, but we had both encouraged it. It's my fault as much as it's yours. If it hadn't been that greasy colonel, it might have been someone else." I paused and stepped farther away from him. Space was important at this moment. "We have to be more careful. He damned well thinks he knows something is going on."

Riley's face hardened, and I knew he agreed with me. "He definitely thinks that. He has no proof though, and you're right, we shouldn't give him any more reason to suspect."

I nodded and gave him a genuine smile. It softened his features. I longed to smooth out the worry lines that still tightened the corners of his eyes and pulled down the corners of his mouth.

"Walk me back to my room, Colonel?" I held out my arm, and he linked his with mine as he led me back to the hotel.

He left me there though and told me he needed to take a walk to clear his head. I nodded. It would do good for me, too, but the tone of his voice informed me that he meant alone. Worry curdled in my stomach at what might be on his mind, but I tried to push it out as I stripped down in my room for the night.

29

Colonel Lang

Nicole was doing much better about this whole thing than I was. Fury raged within me, and though I desperately wanted to let her console me in her arms, I knew that would only further our problems.

I walked her back to the hotel with only the light of the streetlights to guide our path. It was almost romantic if we didn't give such a wide berth between us. I left her there because the cool night air was just what I needed to clear my head and cool down the two fires burning inside me.

I had to be extra careful on this trip. As Markum's timely arrival hinted, he was certainly keeping a close eye on the two of us. He was fishing for gossip, or anything he could get. Markum was one of those people who longed to have dirt on everyone, and I knew it was to his great frustration that, up until now, I had walked unbendingly on the straight and narrow.

Once the winds swept away what was left of the heat inside me, I made my way back to the hotel. I was happy Nicole found him creepy and greasy. She had a good sense about people, and I hoped her instincts would continue to help her in avoiding him. Once I was back inside my room. I stripped down to my boxer briefs and lay back on the bed and pulled out my phone to message Nicole.

Me: I wish I could come over and finish what we started. Markum's appearance has got me paranoid. We should probably be on our best behavior in case we're being watched.

I dropped the phone and lay back, staring at the ceiling and wondering if she was doing the same. My phone chimed a moment later, and I picked it up. Nicole had sent a frowny face, but the next message stirred my cock.

Nicole: That's disappointing. I wanted to be bad.

It was far from within my ability to tell her no. Even after my internal pep talk about avoidance. I chuckled and pushed off my boxer briefs and commanded her to do the same with her panties. Once she informed me she was completely undressed, I sent her a video chat. She answered quickly and greeted me with a sexy smile.

"That's better." I returned her smile. "Now keep the phone where I can see your face, and take your other hand, and finish what I started before we were so rudely interrupted."

She adjusted her position as she bit her lip and reached down between her legs. The thought of seeing her face when she came had me hard instantly. She let out a pleased moan as she stroked herself, and my cock twitched, so I grabbed it and stroked myself as well.

"Try to keep your voice down if you can. I don't want anyone in the hallway getting too interested in what you're doing."

She raised her eyebrows as she challenged me, and I wished I could pin her down and kiss those mischievous lips.

"Oh, God, Nicole. You look so fucking hot when you're pleasuring yourself. I wish I could see the whole of you."

She smiled and leaned the phone so I got a quick flash of her breasts, but then, I could clearly see the apex between her legs and the way her fingers toyed with her clit before sliding inside her.

It didn't take long before she was panting and the video was shaking. She moved the phone back up so that it was looking at her face, and my breath quickened with hers. She bit harder on her lip as she squirmed and bucked.

"Let me hear you cum, Nicole, that's an order," I commanded, and she cried out as her hips flew up and the phone fell out of her hand. All I could do was hear her after that, but it didn't matter because my cock twitched, and I came soon after.

After she calmed down, she grabbed the phone so we could stare at each other as we caught our breaths.

I smiled adoringly at her. "You're so beautiful when you come, Goddamn it."

"I heard you come, too, Riley, that was hot. I can't wait until you do that inside me."

I let out a throaty laugh as arousal snuck over me again at her words. She had the ability to do that to me like no woman had before. There was no way I could come again today, though. I was too jetlagged.

"You drive me wild, woman. You're irresistible." She blushed but smiled at me. "Now, you actually have to get to sleep. Tomorrow is going to be a long day."

She nodded and wished me a good night as she hung up. I cleaned myself up before crawling back into bed. It felt so disappointingly empty without her there, and I wondered if she thought the same. Despite the loneliness, I was tired enough after our day that sleep came over me quickly. I drifted off with thoughts of her on my mind.

30

Sergeant Massey

The next couple days were dreadfully boring. We were stuck in meetings and seminars round the clock, and by the time we stumbled into our rooms, we collapsed in our own beds and slept.

The days dragged on with meaningless small talk, painfully polite smiles, and stiff handshakes. I looked forward to seeing the colonel, but he treated me with professional indifference as his secretary as we navigated through the crowds.

I dutifully took notes and religiously avoided Markum, which was increasingly more difficult the busier that Riley got. Markum seemed to find a way to work himself into all my side conversations and caught me whenever I drifted away from the group to grab a drink or snack. His persistence was irritating and exhausting rather than endearing, as he seemed to think it was.

I hoped Riley and I would have another chance for dinner or a video call, but he had been pulled into long conversations after the meetings finished or went out for drinks with the guys.

Though I understood the necessity of maneuvering through the political landscape, it still left me feeling bummed as I hadn't gotten so much as a wanting look or a saucy text message even through the flight back home. My "Good night, sir" text was met with "Good night, Sergeant" or no response at all.

It was probably for the best that we kept some distance, and he had probably been incredibly careful since our close call the first night. But I missed him already.

On the flight back, I swore I felt his eyes on me, but when I tried to meet them, he would look away immediately. I resisted the urge to reach out and brush my hand over his. It wasn't a particularly long flight, so I chastised myself and kept my hands to myself, resigned to staring out the window and suppressing the need to longingly sigh.

Once we got to his car and he still hadn't met my eyes or touched me, I began to grow worried. I almost didn't notice the way his knuckles desperately gripped the steering wheel or that he was going far over the speed limit. Once he put the car in park in his driveway, he dragged me over the seat to him and captured my lips in a quick, searing kiss. I melted against him, but before I could glue myself to him, he pulled away.

"Go up to my room right now and undress. That's an order," he demanded, and I walked after him up the stairs, his intensity shocking me into obedience.

I followed his example and stripped what I could along the way, so by the time we were to the bed, I was tossing the necessities to the floor. He pulled me against him immediately, rocking me until I was pinned underneath him on the bed. His lips were pure fire against mine. His hands explored my body, and the passion reminded me much of our first time together.

His thumb stroked over my nipples and I arched into him, spreading my legs wide as he settled between them. He rocked against me, teasing his cock at my entrance and I whimpered as I wrapped my legs around his waist, encouraging him. I needed him. I needed this.

"God, how I missed you," he moaned against my lips as he guided himself inside me.

He sheathed himself completely and captured my moan with his kiss. I hummed against him as I held him there. I hadn't realized how empty I felt without him there to fill me. He finally pulled away and pinned my hands above my head as he fell into a steady rhythm. He slid in and out of me with delicious friction, and it unraveled me. My core was throbbing, and as he pushed himself completely into me one more time, we peaked together.

Warmth filled me as my muscles clenched around him, and I moaned without restraint. He collapsed on top of me as we caught our breaths and came down from our highs. I had missed him so desperately. My body still wanted more even as it ached from having gone without sex for several days. He rolled over onto his side next to me and traced his fingers lazily over my stomach as he admired me.

I stared at him dreamily with my arms still stretched above me, twisted into his sheets. He kissed me softly, and his fingers danced lightly over my skin before sliding between my legs. I eagerly spread my legs for him and let him work his magic on me. He had me quivering in a matter of minutes, and just after I came, his cock was ready for another round. By the time he was finished with me, my whole body ached even more, and I blissfully descended into sleep in his arms.

31

Sergeant Massey

The week went by remarkably fast due to the conference, and I was happy to wake up on Friday and know the whole weekend would be spent in Riley's arms and in bed. I was zinging all morning, trapped in the clouds, as I hummed to myself as I made my way to the restroom at the office. Someone came down the hallway towards me, but I didn't notice them until they blocked my path into the restroom.

"You sure look happy for a Friday."

His voice jerked me out of my reverie, and I met the hungry eyes of Colonel Markum. The happiness drained from my face as his gaze ran up and down my body. I was wearing my fatigues today, and his look made my skin crawl. He was standing far too close to me for comfort. I went to step back, but he grabbed my arm.

"Did you forget that tight little number from the other day?"

"Oh, no, sir, I haven't had the time to get a new uniform, but I won't be wearing that again." I narrowed my eyes, trying to yank out of his grip, but his fingers tightened almost painfully.

"That's a shame. Your ass looked wonderful in it." He paused a moment as his stare lingered on my breasts. I cleared my throat and he met my eyes with a smirk. "Sorry, I was just admiring you. Maybe if Riley let you off the leash once in a while…" He trailed off and reached out with his free hand to grab a strand of my hair. "Keeping you all to himself behind closed doors when you should be out enjoying the rest of world."

His words pissed me off, and I set my jaw as I glared at him. "I'm sorry, but I'm not sure what you're talking about. Now, if you'll excuse me, I'll be getting on my way." I yanked on his grip again, my fists clenching as I prepared to abandon my politeness.

Markum sneered and pulled me into him. "Oh, I don't think Riley will miss you just yet."

"Excuse me—" I started, but he glanced around me before dragging me into the empty ladies' room and locking the door behind him.

An icy chill went down my spine as my heart pounded in my chest. He had me alone, and though I was stronger than most women and Markum was hefty, he was still taller and stronger. My brain raced along with my heart for options, but he quickly grabbed me and shoved me up against the door, groping my breasts roughly and leaning in for a kiss.

He reeked of cigarettes and sweat, and as I struggled, he locked my hands together with his and pinned them above me. His tongue forced its way into my mouth, and I gagged as I squeaked and pushed against him. He seemed to have misread my squirming away from him as rubbing against him as he pressed harder against me, his erection poking my lower abdomen.

Fear and disgust mixed in my stomach, and I tried to scream, but he covered my mouth quickly with a hand. He leaned into me with a smirk on his face and pressed his lips against my ear.

"You like that, don't you, you little slut…"

I heaved my body weight against him but only succeeded in removing his hand from my mouth. "No, I don't, get off me and leave me alone, you fucking pervert," I cursed at him.

I tried to scream for help, but he covered my mouth again, his eyes wild with fury. Tears stung my eyes, threatening to fall as he ripped open my shirt, buttons clattering to the ground as his free hand dove under my T-shirt to grope me.

"Come on, you let the big Colonel Lang have a taste, why not share the goods with me?" he whined, and my eyes were wide with fear as I pushed against him.

He let go of my arms and brought his hand down to cup my face, and I bit down on it hard, blood filling my mouth, and he cursed, releasing me for a moment.

"I said get off, you creep." I turned and grabbed the handle but forgot the door was locked.

By the time I was reaching for the lock, Markum had grabbed me again and yanked me back, smacking me against the far wall. His eyes were cold as he let out ragged breaths as he made his way towards me. "Is that how you speak to your superior officer?" His hands squeeze my breasts with bruising grips.

I cried out as a sob raked me. "Please, please just let me go, and I won't say anything to anyone," I begged, tears streaking my cheeks. "Please."

His grip didn't let up as he continued to fondle me before pressing himself against me and kissing me roughly. I pushed against him, but his grip was stronger now.

"You're not going to say anything to anyone at all, and even if you did, no one would believe you. I tried to do this the nice way, but now, we're going to do this the hard way. I'm going to ruin your career, and then, I'm going after Riley. Don't think I haven't noticed how he looks at you. You're fucking him, and it's time to give me a piece of the pie."

His hands found my pants, and I screamed out as he fumbled with the button. He slapped me, and the shock left me slightly dazed and silent and sniffling a moment.

This isn't happening. This isn't happening. I kept repeating the same thought, but all my senses were assaulted by him as I started sobbing again. I scratched at him, but he tore out my button and ripped down my zipper. I smashed my head against his, and he stumbled back as I lunged for the door. He grabbed my legs and knocked them out from under me, pinning me beneath him.

"Please help me, please!" I cried out towards the door, but he dragged me back towards him, pulling my pants down as he did so. I sobbed and screamed as I kicked back at him.

"Shut up! This is all your fault, you know. You asked for this. Teasing me with that tight little skirt. I saw the way you wanted me, the way you smiled at me. Now, you're going to give me what I want. Maybe, I'll let Riley know how much you begged for it. I bet he won't be able to look at you again."

"No, please, I didn't mean to, I didn't," I begged.

He flipped me so that he was straddling me. He grabbed my throat, crushing my windpipe and silencing me. I gasped for breath, swatting at his hands to release me, but he was too strong.

Underneath the door, I saw shadows move in the light. *Help. Please help.* Black spots clouded my vision as my breathless pleas went unheard. *No!* I wouldn't go down like this.

I somehow found the strength to move him over enough to bring a leg up, and I pushed against the floor hard, moving Markum off me enough for me to bring my knee up into his groin. He bowed over, groaning as he cupped himself. I scrambled to my feet, my breaths ragged and painful, and made a mad dash for the door.

I turned the lock and grabbed the knob when he yanked my feet out from under me again and pulled me back towards him. I kicked and scratched at him, but he got to his feet and began to kick me. He got a good one in my side that knocked the breath out of me. I tried to scream as his foot came toward my head, but it all went black.

32

Colonel Lang

It was by some miracle that the military police showed up just before I ground Markum's face into the concrete wall. I paced the waiting room, fuming, desperately wanting to see her. I missed the ambulance ride when the other officers were questioning me about what happened. When I found Markum poised over Nicole's unconscious body, my first thought through the red haze was that I wanted blood.

One of the other women in our corridor had come to my office to tell me there was a commotion in the bathroom. Panic gripped me tightly as I dashed to the restroom where Nicole had excused herself to.

The door was stuck, but I managed to force it open. Markum had his pants down and Nicole's were at her ankles when he looked up and gave me a malicious grin. Her top was spread open and her T-shirt pulled up, exposing her bra. She was completely still, and I noticed the blood dripping from her nose as a nasty bruise bloomed on her face. I knocked Markum off her as I pulled her pants up and then pulled her shirt down.

"Now, now, Riley. She asked for it. Said she loved it a little rough."

I don't remember asking for the police or for an ambulance, but according to the witnesses, I did. I do remember grabbing Markum and slamming him into the wall and pounding my fist into his skull. My ears were ringing, and I didn't hear anything he spat at me until the police pulled me off. He was probably lucky I couldn't, or I wouldn't have been able to resist the urge to keep punching until there was nothing left. I wasn't the calm and contained Colonel Lang everyone at the base had known. I was running only on primal rage as they watched me bash another man's head into the wall.

I'd damned near hit the police officer who grabbed my shoulder to stop me. I stepped back to give them space.

Markum's face was barely recognizable, but apparently, he could still speak because he called out. "I warned you that you couldn't keep her all to yourself."

The officers had enough sense to duck when I got one last punch in that left him slumped over. My hand was battered and bruised as well, but I thought of nothing as I kneeled next to Nicole. The crowd gathering at the door pissed me off more, and I blocked their view of her as I glared at them.

"What the fuck are you all doing? Get out of here and give her some damn privacy."

They also had enough sense to disperse as the police dragged Markum's limp body out and reinforcements showed up to question witnesses. They got to me last as I checked over Nicole and cooed at her in desperation to wake her up. At least, she was breathing, even if the breaths were shaky.

The paramedics arrived the same time they were trying to question me. I gave them a quick description and they rolled her away as the police held me back. I held my tongue about our relationship, but I left out no detail about the way Markum had been harassing her. The woman who had come to get me verified my story, so they allowed me to leave to see to the condition of my subordinate.

When I arrived at the hospital, the nurses informed me Nicole was still being checked out and wasn't in a condition for visitors. I felt unsettled now knowing what was going on, so I paced back and forth in the waiting room.

A kindly older nurse approached and asked to treat my hand, but when I shook my head, she nodded and left me alone. I would bury Markum so deep in the ground that even his name would never surface.

My hands clenched into fists again and I couldn't contain my rage. I spun around and punched the nearest wall. Something in my hand popped and I cursed loudly, cradling it to me, as I gritted my teeth. I was naïve to think Markum wasn't such a low piece of dirt. I shouldn't have stopped hitting him. No one would have blamed me for it. Though that wasn't always true with the military, I had enough of a good reputation that it would have blown over eventually. I should have done that for her. How could I even look her in the eye after I failed to protect her?

Tears stung my eyes in both anger and disappointment in myself because I failed her.

My hand had swollen dangerously by the time the nurse returned and pestered me enough that I let her look at it. Apparently, I fractured it in two places. It was a quick fix with a light cast, and I shrugged off the pain meds as I waited for them to let me in to see Nicole.

If she decided she didn't want to see me again, that was up to her, but otherwise, I pledged never to leave her side again. Rules and regulations be damned. I had been in the military for twenty years and played by the book for long enough. Nicole was mine, and if I had to declare that to deter the vultures, then I would make sure every asshole who ever glanced her way again knew it.

Finally, after a couple hours of waiting, they said she would be waking up soon. I demanded they let me back to be with her. The nurse stared at my hand and shook her head. I felt as if I had been struck as I realized her confusion. I held up my hand to show her.

"This is what I did to the asshole that did that to her. Please let me see her. She's my girlfriend."

My pleading eyes must have led her to finally cave. She led me back, and I stood in the doorway a moment. The breath sucked out of my lungs as I stared at her. She looked sincere, and I was just thankful for a moment that she was still alive.

"What's her condition," I asked breathlessly, biting back the tears, and the nurse grabbed her chart.

"Severe bruising on her breasts, thighs, ankles, and upper arms. Her windpipe was damaged, and there's dark bruises caused from strangulation. She has a couple fractured ribs and probably a minor concussion, but we won't be able to assess that until she wakes up. There are no signs of forced penetration, so you must have showed up just before, but she's in a pretty rough state still. I can't imagine what that poor girl went through. You take care of her, all right."

I nodded, but I tuned her out after that as I went over to sit by Nicole's side. The nurse checked the machines before leaving us alone. I waited until her footsteps disappeared before I grabbed Nicole's hand in mine and finally allowed myself to cry.

33

Sergeant Massey

My head fucking hurt. That was my first thought as the grogginess transitioned into blooming pain from my skull. There was a dull throbbing in my ribs, but it was barely noticeable compared to the pounding of my head. It hurt to think. It hurt to breathe. What the hell did I do to myself?

I groaned as the confusion faded and I began to register my surroundings. A steady beeping drummed on and someone shifted near me, a chair creaking underneath them.

"Nicole, baby, can you hear me?" Hands, gentle and warm, pressed against my face.

I knew that voice. I tried to open my eyes, but the fluorescents were piercing causing my headache to throb harder. I drew in a sharp gasp and flinched.

"Hold on, I'll close the door and shut the lights off."

The hands left, and I let out a pained whimper, but it was more of a croak due to the dryness of my throat. He returned, and I peeked again to find soothing darkness. Light streamed in through cracks from the window blinds, but it was semi-bearable as my eyes adjusted. I met the concerned, handsome face of Colonel Lang. I tried to smile, but the action hurt, and I hissed at the pain. He went to say something, but the door opened, light blinding me for a moment, but it was easier to adjust this time. A woman walked in, and the colonel met her at the end of the bed.

Their muffled voices were hard to sort through and concentrating only further exacerbated the pounding. I caught snippets, though, like the words assault and trauma. I struggled to remember what had happened, but I only got to the part where I popped in on Riley to tell him I was going to stop by the bathroom quickly before we left for lunch when the woman walked over to me.

"Nicole, I'm Dr. Brenden. I need to check you over to make sure you don't have a concussion." Her voice wasn't nearly as soft and soothing as Riley's.

I glanced over at him, and he nodded, moving to the other side of the bed from the doctor and grabbing my hand. I opened my mouth to speak, but my throat ached, and the only sound that came out was garbled noises.

She frowned so I just gave a slight nod and winced. She leaned over me and lightly prodded the side of my skull, and when she brushed her finger over my right cheekbone, overwhelming pain shot through me, and I jerked away from her touch, black spots dotting my vision. She made a comment to the attending nurse that I couldn't hear before she turned back to me. She pulled something out of her pocket and shined a bright light in my eyes that left me blinded. I decided I was not a fan of her at all.

"Her reactions are normal. I'll prescribe her some meds for the pain and some to reduce the swelling," she said to the colonel before turning her attention to me. "Nicole, you just rest up for now, and I'll come check on you in the morning. Try not to speak too much to give your vocal cords a rest. They need a break, and what you need most of all is sleep."

She mentioned something to Riley, and he nodded before she left. The nurse came in a moment later and injected something into my IV. Riley waited until she left before he looked down at me. I noticed the exhaustion etched into his face. Dark circles bloomed under his eyes and the stubble on his cheeks was unkempt. He didn't meet my eyes as he stroked his thumb over the back of my hand.

"Markum will pay for what he did to you. I promise you, Nicole. I will never let anything happen to you so long as I live. Men like him will be punished to the fullest extent of the law."

At the mention of his name, the memories flooded in like horrible little flashes as the blanks in my memory filled.

Panic set my heart racing and the monitor beeped louder as I stared up at Riley in horror. *Oh God. Oh God. Markum tried to… Did he… Oh God…* I covered my mouth with my hand and tears stung at my eyes. I tried to speak, to ask him if Markum finished what he started, but it came out as a horrible wheezing noise that left me startled.

"It's okay, baby, don't try to talk. You're safe now. I won't leave your side. Just get some sleep."

Tears streamed down my cheeks, and Riley reached down to gently cradle my face with his hands as he carefully wiped them away. He whispered soothing words to me, and I nuzzled against him. Whatever the nurse gave me must have finally kicked in because I allowed sleep to whisk me away.

*****

Markum was in my dreams. He watched me as I stumbled forward, laughing as I glanced behind me and prayed he wouldn't find me. His sneering face appeared around every corner as I ran through the endless maze of hallways. Running, desperately running. I knew he was chasing me, and I never seemed to be running fast enough; his loud footsteps were constantly behind me, taunting me.

I saw a door at the end of the hallway. A light at the end of the tunnel, and I knew, I just knew, Riley was waiting on the other side. I reached for the knob, but it disappeared. I screamed in frustration and banged on the door, but it disappeared along with the floor as I was sucked into the darkness. His laugh echoed, and the last thing I saw before it all went black was his face.

The second time I woke up was easier. The world was fuzzy around the edges, and I knew they had given me something because the pain was thoroughly dulled.

Riley had been sleeping in the chair next to my bed, his head resting against my leg, and when I stirred, he woke up. He immediately grabbed my hand and pulled it to his lips to give it a soft kiss. I swallowed, and my throat felt like a desert.

"Water," I croaked, happy that the noises coming from my throat were words rather than gurgles.

Riley immediately stood and grabbed a glass off the tray at the end of the bed. I tried to lean forward to grab it, but the flash of pain in my ribs caused me to gasp and fall back. He used the remote to recline me and helped me drink. The rush of cool water brought with it an immense relief but also, in my hydrated state, my eyes stung with tears. I grabbed Riley's hand in mine with a death grip to cover the trembling.

"Did he… Did he…" I could have started the sentence a few more times, but when I realized I couldn't bring myself to say that four-lettered-R-word, I just looked at Riley with watery eyes.

"No, no, he didn't. Someone heard the commotion and came to get me. I got to him before he could."

"Oh, thank God." I cried in relief and started to sob, a horrible noise as air was dragged in and out of me roughly, sounding garbled and choked with my damaged vocal cords.

"Oh, Nicole, I could have killed him. I would have. I was about to when the police pulled me off him, but God, how I wanted to. I still wish I did. When I stormed in there, it was all I could think about. He hurt you and took advantage of you, and I wanted him to pay."

Riley sank into the chair next to me, and I looked over at him. He had his face in his hands, and the way his voice shook when he spoke told me he was crying, too.

I noticed his hand was wrapped up, and I reached out and grabbed it, pulling it towards me. It was clenched in a fist, and I kissed each finger until they relaxed. There were so many emotions swirling inside me that I distracted myself with my physical health.

"How long was I out?"

"A few days. There was a lot of swelling in your face and they were worried about swelling in the brain, so they tried to keep you under longer. Fortunately, that's looking much better all around."

"When can I leave then?"

"We'll know more in the morning when the doctor gives you another checkup."

As if on cue, a nurse walked in. She checked my vitals and asked me a couple questions about how I was feeling. She injected something into my IV drip and prescribed me more rest before leaving. I waited until she was out of the room before I looked at Riley.

"How could I have been sleeping for days and still feel tired?"

I used the remote to lower myself back down and yawned, wincing as pain shot out from my cheek and windpipe.

Riley sat in the chair beside me and grabbed my hand again. It felt safe with him there. The bandage wrapping his hand was a visible representation he wouldn't hesitate to protect me. I looked at him as the drugs began to take effect. "I don't think I'll be wanting to go back to work for a while," I manage to say as I fought the urge to fall directly asleep.

"Your boss is a hard-ass, but I think he'll understand. We'll talk about it later. For now, you just focus on getting better."

I gave him a small smile and closed my eyes as drowsiness wrapped around me. I was floating on a cloud, but before I floated away, I mumbled, "Thank you."

34

Colonel Lang

When Nicole woke up again, she finally showed the raggedness one would expect from her injuries and recovery. Dark circles bloomed under her eyes and her skin was pale, bruised along the side of her face that Markum's foot impacted.

In a way, she looked better. The blue and purple bruises were fading to yellow, but it looked mean against her pale skin.

She nodded distantly as the doctor went over her injuries and ran her through the medications she would need to take. She signed her release paperwork and gave me permission to be her caretaker. Her clothes were torn and bloodied, so when the nurse had forced me to go home to get myself sorted, I had packed clothes for both of us.

Every time Nicole winced as they moved her from the bed to the wheelchair, guilt and protectiveness overwhelmed me. I wished Markum was here so I could properly vent my frustration once more.

They were reducing her pain meds to prepare for her departure, and it was showing in the exhausted, aching way she held herself, favoring her right, unbruised side.

I got her into the car and drove us home. She didn't look at me, just stared out the window so I couldn't see her. When I asked her if she wanted anything on the way home, she just sniffled, wiped her cheeks, and asked for her bed. It broke my heart, and I gripped the steering wheel hard enough to turn my knuckles white and make my wrapped hand ache.

"Do you want me to do anything, or do you want me to go?" I asked, trying not to push her beyond her comfort.

She didn't look at me, but I noticed the way she curled up tighter on her bed, as if suddenly more self-conscious about her vulnerability. "What do you want to do?" she asked.

"Honestly, I'd like to lay next to you until you fall asleep."

There was a breath's long pause as she thought. "I'd like that," she whispered so lightly it was a miracle I heard it.

I pulled off my shoes and slid into the bed behind her. I gave her a bit of space as I didn't know how close she would want me. She tried to scoot back into me and drew in a sharp breath as her ribs protested. I quickly moved closer to her and put my arm around her, pulling her tightly against me. She sighed in relief, and I brushed my hand down her hair in a soothing motion.

The pain pills still made her drowsy, so she was out soon. I was still wide-awake, though, so I stayed with her for another ten minutes before I reluctantly dragged myself away.

I went downstairs to her kitchen. Though I had only been inside Nicole's place a few times before, I knew my way around. I went to the fridge to check on her food situation and was knocked back by a putrid odor and a hoard of takeout containers. I shook my head and found some garbage bags and began cleaning out her fridge. When I finished, the leftover ingredients were pitiful. I needed to go shopping.

I brought the garbage to the dumpster and then drove to the store to stock up. I grabbed some of the fruits and veggies I knew she liked as well as a few cans of soup in case she needed something quick. I also replaced the basics—bread, cheese, and milk—and bought food for dinner. Finally, as I walked through the bakery towards the checkout, I saw a display of espresso cupcakes for sale. I grabbed one for Nicole, hoping it would cheer her up.

I put the groceries away when I got back to her house and got a white chicken chili started in the Crock Pot. By the time I finished preparing everything, it was early afternoon, and I knew I couldn't put off the inevitable any longer.

I found some scratch paper lying around and wrote her a note that there was food in the fridge, dinner in the pot, and that she needed to take it easy—that was an order!

I added that I would check on her later and to call me if she needed anything at any point. I left the note on her nightstand with a bottle of water, her phone, and her next dosage of pain pills. I kissed her lightly on the forehead before retreating to my car.

Unfortunately, while I'd like to have stayed with her indefinitely, it was already the middle of the week, and in addition to my normal work, I had the MPs to answer to. I could only avoid them for so long. Plus, the sooner I spoke to them, the sooner Markum would be sentenced and the more secure I'd feel. My testimony would likely be enough to keep them off Nicole's back and still get Markum put away for a long time. I would go take care of that and some errands that needed my immediate attention before I returned in a couple hours to check on Nicole and make her dinner.

I also needed to get the remainder of her enlistment sorted. If I had my way, she wouldn't ever have to set foot on the base ever again.

35

Sergeant Massey

When I finally woke up from my nap after returning home from the hospital, I felt miserable and groggy, inside and out. The sun was still out, but my phone told me it was early evening already. The pills had helped me sleep, I hadn't had any nightmares since the last one I had at the hospital, but it did nothing for clearing out the cloudiness in my head. I briefly remembered the doctor explaining my regiment to me, but I prayed she had written it down somewhere.

Ignoring the throbbing in my ribs and skull, I pushed myself into a sitting position and let my feet dangle off the bed. I sniffed the air, and a delicious scent wafted in. I wondered if Riley was downstairs cooking. Whatever it was, I wanted some.

I noticed the gifts from my Riley on my nightstand when I retrieved my phone and smiled to myself as I glanced over at them again.

I popped the pills, chugged down the water, and then read the note. It made me feel warm on the inside. He probably had an aneurysm when he saw the plethora of takeout containers and my slim pickings of ingredients. I smiled and shook my head at the thought. I was certainly in for a lecture later.

I carefully slid out of bed, my legs shaky but holding my weight. It seemed like every part of me ached, and I was horrified when I tried to try to remember the last time I showered. The fear of me looking as bad as I felt had me avoiding looking into the mirror as I got the shower started.

After I had completely stripped out of my clothes, I finally got a look at my body. Angry yellow and purple bruising trailed up my ribs as well as over my thighs and ankles. I tried not to dwell on it as I turned on the shower and stepped into the warm stream.

I stood under the soothing torrent of water until I began to wrinkle. I wrapped myself in a towel and wiped the foggy surface of the mirror to finally get a look at myself. I drew in a sharp breath as I took in the nasty coloring on my swollen cheek and over my nose. I shook my head. I looked horrible. No amount of concealer would do much to help with this. My eyes trailed down to my neck and froze as panic set in. The bruising on my neck was as dark as the bruises on my face, but the shocking part was the clear handprints on my skin.

I began to shake as tears streamed down my cheeks. I dashed from the bathroom and grabbed my phone before ducking into my closet to have some privacy.

I assumed Riley wasn't here as he'd probably have checked on me after the shower shut off. It gave me some amount of relief that he wouldn't come across me in the middle of my freak-out, but I missed him.

I pulled out my phone and wrote up a few messages before I finally calmed down enough to settle on an appropriate one to send.

Me: Thanks for the food. You didn't have to do that, though.

I barely set the phone back in my lap before it chimed.

Riley: You must eat. Plus, it's no trouble to take care of my woman.

I smiled as a warming glow spread from my chest and tears stung my eyes again. He called me his woman. We hadn't gone so far as saying the L-word to one another, nor had we ever really had a conversation about what we were to one another. I had tried to limit my view of our relationship to just something fun to pass the time with, but I knew my heart tugged me towards more. I had been denying it for a long time, but deep down, I knew it was so much more than just great sex.

Sometimes, I felt like I barely knew him, but as much of a mystery as he turned out to be, I was irrevocably drawn to him, and I wanted to know everything there was to know about him. Though, the events of the past few days probably had a turbulent flood of emotions battling inside him. I knew it left me unstable, but when I thought about him, he was my rock. I hoped he would still want me after everything that happened.

I replied with a thank you and smiley face before feeling content enough to leave the safety of my spontaneous panic room. I made my way to the kitchen and was flustered to find it completely stocked with food cooking on the stove.

I sputtered when I opened the fridge to find all the fixings of a balanced diet and my takeout containers disposed of. They were probably hopelessly spoiled and the task to toss it wouldn't have been an easy one.

A flush of embarrassment crept over my cheeks until my eyes rested on a container on the counter. I approached it, and my heart fluttered. A cupcake, perfectly staged, occupied the container and next to it was a note that read:

A little more sugar for the sweetness in my life.

I hiccupped a sob and pulled the note to my chest. It was so preciously cheesy it had me melting. These simple romantic gestures were powerful, like an arrow straight through my heart. I held the note against me and let happy tears fall for a few moments until my phone dinged with another message.

Riley: Make sure you eat. Dinner won't be done until I'm home, but there's cans of soup on the counter. Those pills aren't meant to be taken on an empty stomach.

I rolled my eyes and then laughed when my phone chimed again.

Riley: That's an order!

So bossy.

Me: Don't worry, sir, I'm already standing in the kitchen. I saw the cupcake. You're gonna give me cavities being this sweet…but also, please don't stop.

Sitting on the counter behind the cupcake was a couple cans of soup. I slopped one into a container and popped it into the microwave for a couple minutes while I leaned against the counter.

Riley: I'm glad you liked it. Don't worry. I'll remind you to brush your teeth.

The conversation was so playful that I appreciated him distracting me from the looming truth of what happened. He was showing me he was there for me, while also respecting my need for space to process everything.

As the silence let my thoughts settle again, I wrapped my arms around myself protectively. I remembered attending a high school seminar on domestic abuse and sexual assault. I recognized that victim blaming only harmed recovery, but I couldn't help but revisit the events that transpired. It was impossible not to point out my faults, consider what I could have done differently, and get dragged into a whirlpool of what-ifs. The beeping of the microwave pulled me out of the dark place, and I took my soup to my bed and wrapped myself cozily in my blankets while I ate.

My phone chimed again soon after I had finished my bowl. It was Riley telling me he would be heading home in a couple hours. It was late for a work night, but if he had been with me since the incident, he probably missed quite a lot of work and needed to catch up. I hoped it wasn't too hard without me there to assist him.

The thought of going back to the office left me trembling, but I knew I'd have to do it eventually. I wasn't sure how this sort of case was handled, but my enlistment wasn't over yet, and I probably still had to speak with the MPs about what happened. I hoped Riley wouldn't be punished too severely for what he did to Markum. I guessed from the looks of his hand that he hadn't held back, and while I was grateful, I was also worried.

The military had a reputation of handling these sorts of cases poorly. Riley was more respected around the base, but he had told me Markum had an armory of secrets and a reputation of ruining others with rumors he conjured up. If Markum decided to blackmail those higher up, could Riley's reputation be in danger?

36

Colonel Lang

It was nearly impossible to get absorbed into my work. Between worrying about Nicole being home alone and anger at the memory that the events had transpired just down the hall, I was an emotional wreck. A lot of the projects I had been supporting hit a lull without me in the office, so my workload was a mountain I needed to conquer to get things back on track. I would need to start training a replacement soon and cutting back on my responsibilities if I was hoping to ever retire from this place.

Fortunately, Nicole's organizational system was logical and intuitive, so I wasn't completely lost without her. It pained me to look out and see her desk empty, though. She was the light in what had been becoming a relatively dreary existence.

I had been taking for granted all the time I was able to spend with her before. When my normal time to leave rolled around and passed, I looked longingly at the clock. I shot Nicole a message, offering to stop by and see how she was doing after I got out. She told me she was grateful for the offer, but she was going to take her pills and then probably be out for the rest of the night. I felt a pang of disappointment, but I wished her a good night's rest and jumped half-heartedly back into my work.

The rest of the week, between work and her medicated sleeps, I didn't get a chance to see her much at all. Besides stopping by to do some chores for her around the house and make sure she still had food while she napped, I never really got any insight into how she was doing. I wanted to ask. I needed to know. But I didn't know how to approach the subject. Decades of sensitivity training didn't really prepare you for when the relationship was far from professional.

The weekend came and went. It wasn't until Monday, after another full day of work, when I really felt caught up on paperwork and responding to all the inquiries that came my way.

I went home after stopping by Nicole's. She was awake in a sense, but the glazed look in her eyes told me she had already taken her meds. I sat with her while she watched TV on the couch and fell asleep against me. I carried her back up to bed and cleaned up before I went home to pass out in my own bed. I wanted to curl up beside her but decided she still needed time to heal.

Tuesday morning came too soon, but I had promised Nicole I would drive her back to the hospital for another checkup before they weaned her off the painkillers. She seemed anxious when I picked her up. I could tell she was wearing makeup to try to hide the bruising, but it still peeked through, yellowed and puffy. It angered me to see it, but I felt a small bit of relief it was healing. I tried to pry into how she was doing, but her curt "fine" led me to abandon the conversation.

The doctor gave her the good to go and wrote her a prescription for a weaker painkiller. Before we left, the doctor pulled me aside and warned me she would likely be irritable and short-fused with the new pain killers. She also suggested finding Nicole a therapist as many survivors reintegrate better with counseling. I thanked her for the advice and walked Nicole back to the car.

I drove her home, but she was quiet and still avoiding meeting my eyes. I picked up some food from her favorite takeout place and then dropped her at home. I offered to stick around, but she declined, saying she was just going to eat and sleep it off.

I held my tongue from saying anything else. I watched her disappear into the house and sighed, resting my head on the top of the steering wheel for a moment. I felt like she was distancing herself from me, which was the exact opposite of what I wanted. I hoped she didn't feel like she was burdening me, and I wanted her to always know that I would be there for her.

The next day I sent her a few texts, but her short answers left me feeling unsatisfied. She needed to talk to someone, but for this, a therapist seemed far more appropriate.

I sent out a couple feelers to the VA health services and to a local women's shelter to get the name of a few local therapists. I figured the best thing to do for now was to give Nicole space and avoid prying but keep the channels open to let her come to me when she decided she was ready.

I visited Nicole that evening bringing her something from a local eatery as well as the contact information for a couple nearby therapists. She seemed annoyed when she read the papers but thanked me for the food before closing me out again. Baby steps.

On Wednesday, the MPs came back with another grueling set of questions, but their appearance was followed by the officer overseeing the case. He assured me Markum had all but confessed and the evidence against him was overwhelming.

It was very unlikely that Nicole would need to make an appearance to secure the decision, but they would probably need a statement from her sometime soon to complete the investigation. He promised that a verdict and sentencing could be decided as soon as next Friday and promised to inform me of any developments. I had a few qualms about the military justice system, but they were at least efficient and expedient in their trials.

On Thursday, Nicole called me to ask if I had some availability in the afternoon to drive her to one of the therapists. I quickly rearranged my schedule to take her. She made some small talk on the drive, but it was strained and forced. The office was in the next town over, so after I dropped her off, I spent some time shopping. I bought a pair of boots and something for Nicole before she texted me to come back and get her. She didn't say much, but there was a change in her demeanor.

Friday, I woke up to a text from her. She said she was tired of being a slump and wanted to do something. I thanked the heavens and asked where she wanted to go. She responded she wasn't sure she was ready to be outside around people, but me and a box of pizza might be just what the doctor ordered.

Relief flooded me, and I went to work with a bit of a pep back in my step. Tonight, I would see Nicole, and I would appreciate every moment with her.

37

Sergeant Massey

Five o'clock on the dot, there was a knock on my door. My makeup was finally able to hide most of the bruises on my face and neck, so I opened the door with a little more confidence than I had before this week. I had been working up the courage to see him all day, so I was mostly prepared when I opened the door.

Riley still took my breath away.

He stood there in a formfitting white T-shirt and jeans with a single red rose in one hand and a pizza in the other. His smile was dazzling. It was as if my fantasy had popped right out of my head and landed right in front of me.

My mouth opened and closed in surprise for a moment before I forced it closed again. My eyes appraised him appreciatively before I stepped back and motioned for him to enter.

He handed me the rose as he stepped inside, and the corners of my lips twitched. I drew in a sharp breath as he walked past and I got to appraise his behind, too. He gave me a dark look, and I followed him to the kitchen silently.

"I've missed you at work. I've completely destroyed your organizational system, and I am no longer able to avoid General Abbott's calls," he told me as he pulled a couple plates from the cupboard.

At the mention of work, I froze up and my heartbeat raced. Riley turned, and his eyes widened in concern.

"When do I have to go back?" I asked meekly, breathless, and he quickly put the plates down on the counter and dashed to me to grab my shaking hands and hold them steady.

"Not any time soon, for certain. Not ever again if I have any say in the matter, which as your boss, I have quite a bit of," he assured me, and the breath wheezed out of me in relief as he ushered me to sit at the table.

Awkward silence filled the air in a suffocating cloud, and I was worried I ruined the mood already. *Good going, Nicole.*

He picked up the plates again and set one in front of me and the other in front of the chair next to me. "Sorry, I shouldn't have brought it up."

"No, no, no. It's all right. It's something I've been wondering about so I'm glad we're talking about it." I paused a moment to put a slice of pizza on my plate and I avoided eye contact as I began to pull off toppings to snack on. "I'm also sorry that I've been avoiding you. It just seemed easier to get my bearings by shutting the world out. I was so afraid that you would just treat me like I'm broken or damaged, and I didn't want to think of myself like that.

"I've always wanted to be 'Nicole the strong,' and it was difficult to let you see me being weak. Talking with the therapist helped, so thank you for that. I still have a lot of work to do before I'm really ready to…you know…talk about things."

His hand covered mine, and I looked up at him. His expression was so endearing it took my breath away.

"Of course, Nicole. You can take as much time as you need. I'll be here if it's two days or two years." He smiled and squeezed my hand. My heart ached. "If it makes any difference, I never thought of you as either of those things. I will never think of you that way either. I may be worried about you, but nothing you do could possibly make me think less of you."

I managed a genuine smile and began to stuff my face. I moaned appreciatively, and Riley choked on his pizza, trying to cover it with a cough. I smiled to myself but kept eating.

"I could use a beer," I told him after finishing the first slice and reaching for another one.

He snorted. "Yeah, right. I may not be a medical professional, but I'm still not an idiot. You can't mix painkillers with alcohol. So, no beer for you."

"Couldn't you just make an exception this once?" I asked and batted my eyelashes as I met his eyes. He raised an eyebrow, not fazed at all.

"Yeah, no, not going to happen. No alcohol for you, young lady."

I feigned disappointment, rolling my eyes, and muttered teasingly, "Is that an order, sir?"

His eyes widened, and his nostrils flared a moment. I wondered what he was thinking as I got him riled him up. I hoped it was along the lines of bending me over his knee and giving my ass a good, hard smack, but I kept that to myself.

I wondered if I was moving too fast for my recovery. It had only been a couple weeks since everything happened. However, the therapist said everyone recovered at a different pace and no single method was better than the others.

The therapist also said some people were back on their feet in a couple days while others took years, but the most important thing was to do what was most comfortable and not force anything. Being with Riley was the only thing right now that didn't feel forced. Being with him made me the most comfortable.

Another slice was enough to fill me up, as both my hunger and energy levels had been off since my stay in the hospital, so I waited for him to finish eating before putting both of our plates in the dishwasher. He packed up the leftovers and stored them in the fridge.

Instinctively, I walked over to him and kissed him appreciatively. He seemed surprised at first, but then, his arms wrapped around me and for a moment, I felt like everything was going to be all right. He kept the passion between us at a simmer, as if he was consciously trying to keep things gentle.

"I missed you," I breathily, and he kissed me once more, longingly, but pulled away again when the pot threatened to boil over. I gave him a disappointed look and could see the strain in his eyes.

"I'm trying to be careful," he told me in a low voice, almost warning me as hunger swirled in his eyes.

It only urged me on. I placed my hands on his chest and twisted my fingers into the fabric of his shirt. "I need you," I purred lightly, and his eyes darkened.

"Nicole," he growled.

I frowned, pushing out my lower lip. "Do you not find me attractive anymore?"

Anger flared in his eyes and he pulled me tightly against him, allowing me to feel his hardness through his jeans. "Does this answer your question?" His voice was throaty, pained, and I smirked. "I wanted to give you time to heal."

I nodded slowly, biting my lip, and pulled away from him. I could see he had more to say, but if it was just to reject me, I didn't really want to hear it. I went to the living room.

He followed closely and sat next to me on the couch. "While I'm here, there's something I need to talk about…" He trailed off, and immediately my anxiety spiked.

The conflicting look on his face told me it wasn't an easy discussion, and I knew it must have something to do with what happened. My whole body tensed, and my heartbeat pounded in my ears.

"They want to get your statement for the case."

I reminded myself to breathe. I knew this was coming. I was dreading it, but I had known I was the kingpin to the case against…Markum. Riley reached out to take my hand, and I grabbed his and squeezed. The skin contact seemed to help calm me enough to talk.

"When do I…" I paused as I rephrased the question. "Do I have to go to the base?"

"I don't think that'll be necessary. They can probably meet you here, or we can work out something with your therapist. Someplace you feel comfortable. I won't make you go back to that place ever again if you don't want to. Okay, Nicole?"

I let out a deep sigh of relief and nodded. A stretch of silence lengthened between us, and the gears of my mind turned as I tried to cope with the news.

Maybe, if Riley was there… Maybe, if the therapist was there… Maybe, I could do it. I had a strong support system next to me. My rock. I smiled to myself as Riley took over my thoughts and pushed out the anxiety.

"I wasn't expecting to fall for you."

He glanced up at me in surprise.

"When I saw you in the bar, I thought you were hot, but when I realized you were my supervisor, I was determined to avoid you at all costs.

"I was just going to finish up the remainder of my enlistment and get the hell out of Dodge. With you, though, it was like a game. You were always goading me and tempting me in one way or another. I was so worried of someone finding out, of ending both of our careers.

"Now, I'm completely smitten. I'm in love with you, hopelessly. And I'm pretty sure everyone knows there's something between us, and I'm sorry about that."

"Funny thing is, that's the same way I thought about you. I love you, Nicole. I knew immediately that you were unique, but I never imagined it would go this far." He paused as he reminisced and smiled. "I'm glad it did, though. Don't worry about the other stuff for now, and don't be sorry. I'll take care of things at the base. You just focus on you, okay? Maybe, me, too, a little, when you're up to it."

"I'm up to it now," I told him, my voice a little too breathless to be casual, but I met his eyes anyways.

His eyes widened in surprise a moment before they darkened. "Are you sure?"

I nodded and his eyes were wanting with a primal hunger that left my stomach flipping with anticipation. "I want you, Riley."

"Those are the only words I need to hear." He pulled me up off the couch and escorted me to the bedroom.

38

Colonel Lang

I was second-guessing myself the whole way to the bedroom. Was it healthy for her? Did she really mean it? Would she regret it? But the moment I laid her on the bed, her eyes lit with pure adoration and her legs instinctively spread as I settled between them. I knew that it was all right. That she was going to be okay.

My lips brushed over hers with featherlight touches, and she wrapped her legs and arms around me, pulling me into her. If I had considered her fragile, this was her urging me not to. She locked me into a tight-lipped kiss, and when I pulled away, I grabbed her arms and pinned them above her head.

"There's no need to rush," I murmured between kisses as she panted against me. "We have all night."

This seemed to slow her down as she leaned into me and let me take the lead. I sat up for only a moment to pull off my shirt before capturing her lips again.

My hands traced their way down her sides to the edges of her blouse and slowly slid it up her stomach. I paused when I saw the bruised flesh over her ribs. I frowned and traced my fingers around the edge.

She drew in a sharp breath but in her eyes, I saw no pain, only lust. I pulled the shirt over her head and tossed it aside before I pressed our bodies together and consumed her.

My hands made quick work of our pants and everything underneath until we were both naked. Her hips ground against mine, and I pulled away just far enough to take a moment to admire her.

"I'm going to make love to you, Nicole. I'm going to savor ever moment with you, every taste of you, every sound. I want to take it all in."

Her smile brightened at my words, and my heart panged in my chest. She was certainly like no woman I had ever been with before. Not in the way that she made me feel both sexually and emotionally. It was both terrifying and thrilling.

"Please," she murmured as she closed her eyes and spread her legs wider and her fingers twisted into the sheets above her head.

It was more than enough to drive a man wild. I ran the head of my shaft along the cleft between her legs and traced a kiss up her neck to her ear. I nibbled and nipped and ran my tongue along her sensitive flesh.

She squirmed and whimpered as she rubbed against me, urging me to go deeper. I felt the need to tease her a little longer, so I kissed my way down her neck, nipped at her collarbone, and stopped right at her breasts.

I sucked gently on a nipple as I swirled my tongue around the sensitive flesh. She thrashed underneath me and moaned. I nipped playfully and she jerked, arching her back to rub against me harder. I smiled to myself satisfactorily as I moved to her other breast and gave it a similar treatment. I continued to grind my body against hers and felt her wetness on my lower abdomen.

I groaned and trailed soft kisses down the soft, sensitive skin of her stomach and along the lines of her hips until I found myself at the peak between her thighs.

My fingers traced lazy circles on the inside of her legs as I inhaled her scent. My mouth salivated as I ached to taste her. Nicole lifted her head as if to wonder what I would possibly do next, but as my tongue dipped between her nether lips, brushing the outside of her entrance, she gasped and fell back, grasping at the bedding.

I explored her mound with my tongue until I found her swollen little bud. I flicked my tongue across it, and she cried out, trembling underneath me. She was ready to come undone. I expertly swirled my tongue in figure eights around her clit, and she moaned as she bucked her hips against my face. I felt her getting close, but I pulled away, choosing to lap at her dripping entrance and twist my tongue inside her. Her muscles tightened down on me and I pulled back again. She groaned in frustration.

"Stop teasing me, and just fuck me already," she growled, and I grinned.

I moved up to claim her mouth again so she could taste herself on my lips. Her tongue danced with mine, and she moaned pleasantly.

"I want you inside me."

"You want me inside you what?" I teased, and her brow puckered in frustration.

"Sir," she strained breathlessly. "I want you inside me, sir."

I lined my hardness up at her entrance and slowly pushed in, watching the frustration dissipate into pleasure. That look on her face was all I could think about. It was everything I ever wanted.

Once I was sheathed completely inside her, her tense muscles clenched tightly around me, I paused a moment to admire her.

"What?" She looked puzzled as she glanced into my eyes, and I smiled.

"You're absolutely beautiful, Nicole." Her face reddened in sudden embarrassment and I leaned down to kiss her. "I'm serious. You complete me on so many levels."

She cupped my face in her hands as her muscles shifted around my cock, causing me to shudder for a moment.

"I could say the same about you. Now hurry up and finish what you started…sir."

I grinned and kissed her once more as I started to pull out of her. My next words came out as more of a growl than I intended. "I love you, Nicole."

She wrapped her legs around me, rocking me back into her deeper than before. "I love you, too, Riley."

My heart jumped at her words. I could hear them said a thousand times more and they would have the same breathtaking effect.

I thrust into her deeper and harder as we both approached our peaks. Nicole came before me, but the feeling of her spasming against my cock pushed me over the edge, and I finished deep inside her.

My arms shook as I tried to prop myself above her but I collapsed, careful to roll away from her injured side as I did so. I pulled her into me and rolled on my back as we both calmed down and caught our breaths.

"How are you feeling?" I asked, kissing the top of her head.

She took a deep breath and hummed in satisfaction.

"I feel so much better now," she cooed, and I chuckled, kissing her forehead.

I stayed lying with her for only a moment longer before I decided now was as good a time as any. I was ready for more and to take the next step with her.

I got out of bed and told her to hang tight a minute as I had something for her. Any rational person might have called me crazy, but when it came to her, it was so much more than that.

39

Sergeant Massey

I watched his naked form appreciatively as he walked out the door and I suppressed a giggle. I rolled onto my back and stared up at the ceiling, glowing with the aftereffects of the amazing sex we just had. He was the epitome of male perfection. And he was all mine. He might have been twenty years my senior, but he had taken great care of his body, and I appreciated the view. Especially the view when he returned.

He had a nervous aura around him as he sat down on the side of the bed that made me nervous as well. He had his hands in his lap and was fidgeting with them. I couldn't see his face, so I sat up and kneeled right next to him, putting my hand on his shoulder. He glanced up at me, and his eyes held pure adoration. He cleared his throat and grabbed my hand.

"Nicole, from the moment I first laid eyes on you, I knew there was something about you. I wanted to know everything about you, needed to spend more time with you, and so I got you to work for me. At first it was just casual curiosity. Then it blossomed into so much more. The more time I spent with you, the happier I found myself. Now, I just don't know what I would do without you."

He looked away from me, and a smile flashed across his lips. He turned his other hand over, and in it sat a black, velvet box.

My breath caught in my throat as my heart fluttered. Tears stung my eyes, and my lips trembled. He opened the box and placed it on the bed in front of me. Nestled in the box was a dazzling diamond ring. I covered my mouth and suppressed a sob.

"You have already made me the happiest man in the whole world. I want to spend the rest of my life with you. I want to make you happy, and I never want to stop. I love you and have never been so sure of anything in my life. So, Nicole, will you marry me?"

I nodded as I began to hyperventilate. "Yes, oh God, yes," I managed breathlessly and pressed my face against his shoulder as I began to cry.

Riley chuckled as he grabbed my left hand and slid the ring onto it. He tilted my head up, and I could see the tears welling in his own eyes. He wiped my cheeks dry before leaning in to kiss me. He pulled me up into his lap, wrapped his arms around me, and held me against his chest.

His voice shook as he spoke. "I was devastated when I broke that door down to see that bastard trying to have his way with you. I would have ripped him to pieces."

I felt his body go tense for a moment, and I held tightly onto him.

"You're mine, Nicole. I claim you. You're going to be my wife, and I don't care if the rest of the world knows it. Damn the consequences."

I pressed my lips against his neck and trailed kisses up to his ear as I trembled. "I love you, Riley."

He moved me so that I was straddling him and could feel his hardness throbbing against the inside of my thigh. I smirked and kissed his lips as I rubbed my sex against him. He groaned and guided his shaft into position.

"You're insatiable, sir." I could feel his lips twitch against mine.

"Only for you."

Epilogue

Nicole

Markum didn't get life in prison, but he wasn't going to be bothering anyone for at least the next couple of decades. No matter how many favors he called in, the evidence was too substantial, and Riley fought for me every step of the way. I was able to get out of the army early with an honorable discharge. I also got out of my lease early so that I could move in with Riley.

We got married on a beach in the Caribbean with my mother and one of Riley's army buddies as our witnesses. We spent two weeks there on our honeymoon, but the majority of it we stayed locked in our room, lost in each other.

That was a year ago, and since then, I enrolled in college and am over halfway through my degree. Riley has been talking about retiring but he hadn't decided when yet. He wanted to leave the army but spent the past decade making himself irreplaceable, so they'd been finding every reason in the book to keep him there.

I smiled to myself as I set the table for our anniversary dinner. Riley had been giving me lessons in cooking, and while I was still far from being any semblance of a chef, my cookbook now included more than scrambled eggs and grilled cheese.

I set the casserole on the table and lit the candles. I checked the time and smiled as I heard the familiar whir of the garage door opening. My hand fluttered to the cigar box on the table, and I bit my bottom lip nervously. Still wearing my apron, I greeted him at the door with a kiss, and he pulled me into him as he deepened it and took my breath away. He handed me flowers and spun me around as he led me to the kitchen.

"Something smells delicious. I have news to tell you." He riffled through the cupboards, pulling out two goblets, before pulling a bottle of red wine out of the fridge.

I smiled to myself, anxious to hear what had him beaming but waited until he popped the bottle and handed me a glass. "I have news as well, but you go first."

"Okay, so, tomorrow, I'm going to put in my notice of retirement. They are dragging their feet on deciding on a date that works best for them, so I'm giving them a hard deadline. I'm thinking either a few months, when I finish my twenty-fourth year, or maybe waiting one more year to make it twenty-five. Then you would be graduated, and it would give us a little time to ourselves and to figure out where we want to move to. I wanted to ask your opinion before I made it official."

"Before you decide, you should open your gift from me." I smiled, and he raised a curious eyebrow. I grabbed the cigar box and handed it to him.

He opened it, and inside were two cigars—one with a pink band and one with a blue band. He stared at them for a long moment before looking back up at me with soft eyes. "How far along are you?"

"About two months. I should be able to finish this semester, and then, most of my courses can be taken online, so I'll be able to stay home and finish it up."

He took the wine from me and set it on the table before he grabbed me up in his arms and spun me around. I laughed, and he kissed me sweetly.

"I'll tell them I won't be making it to twenty-five. I want to be home with you and the baby." He lowered himself down onto his knees. He kissed my belly and looked up at me with tears in his eyes. "I'm going to be a father."

Tears streamed down my cheeks, and he quickly stood to catch them, brushing them away with a sweep of his thumbs. He left me for a moment to put the casserole back in the oven on a low temperature and grabbed my hand.

"Dinner can wait. I'm going to make love to my beautiful wife."

He swept me off my feet, and I squealed in surprise and laughed as he carried me up to the bedroom and laid me down on the bed.

"I love you, Nicole."

"I love you, too, Riley."

And I lost myself in him once again.

About J. Raven Wilde

J. Raven had spent most of her life traveling around the US or abroad, managing to find a bookstore in every city she visited. She began writing when she was a little girl, and it slowly grew into something she loved doing.

Now that she isn't traveling as much anymore, she spends her time writing steamy romance stories at her quiet modest home by the lake.

Connect with J. Raven Wilde

If you loved this story, sign up to receive J. Raven's newsletter at www.TwistedCrowPress.com. Subscribers get the latest information on cover reveals, new or upcoming releases, and promos. Plus, it's FREE, and she promises never to spam you or give out your information. You can also follow her on her Facebook Group, Wilde Raven's Steamy Reads.